BLACKTHORN

AIMÉE CHALMERS

– LUMPHANAN PRESS 2013 –

Self-published in 2013 with the aid of Lumphanan Press
Roddenbrae, Lumphanan, Aberdeenshire, AB31 4RN

www.lumphananpress.co.uk

Marion Angus illustration (page 7) by John Strachan.

ISBN: 978-0-9927468-0-3

Typset in Minion Pro

This book is for my beloved man.

MARION ANGUS
(1865 - 1946)

Marion Angus, a daughter of the manse, grew up in Arbroath, Angus. She was a fine lyrical poet who struggled throughout her life to maintain her commitment to her writing, due to economic and social circumstances beyond her control. Sadly, these very circumstances (poverty, homelessness and caring responsibilities), that so readily destroy self-esteem and self-confidence, are as prevalent in society now as they were in the early 20th century.

It was lack of evidence about the early years of Marion's adulthood, her reticence in later years, and her poetry, which engages the reader at a deep psychological level, that enabled the male literary elite, after Marion's death, to characterise her as 'an elderly spinster who communed with fairies'. But research for *The Singin Lass: Selected work of Marion Angus* (Polygon, 2006) which provides an overview of Marion's life and work, revealed that in her youth Marion was spirited, vivacious and lively. She loved outdoor sports, walked the hills, travelled in Europe, wrote with wit about literature, the theatre, music and philosophy.

ABOUT BLACKTHORN

෴

Blackthorn presents a credible alternative to the inaccurate assumptions previously written about Marion Angus. Less of a fictional biography, more of a novel, it draws on actual family circumstances as well as on Marion's youthful passions. About the nature of love; about duty; about fate – enchantment, enigma, coincidence; it questions how we ever know the 'truth'. Is it through 'experts', friends, art... or some inner sense?

Would Marion appreciate *Blackthorn's* challenge to the stereotyping that cast her as one-dimensional? Would she welcome the respect shown in *Blackthorn* for her resilience, her celebration of the land, her accomplished use of the Scots tongue? Perhaps she would. In her own first public literary venture – 'diaries' written for the 'Arbroath Guide' – fictional and real characters mingle. In them, she constantly challenges the social mores of her times, in particular the attitude towards women. Calculation and scientific certainty were of less interest to her than mystery. Her poetry and prose is full of romantic 'hints and possibilities' – and moonlight.

March 3rd 1899
And if some curious searcher after things forgotten lights on this old Diary of mine, and smiles at the thoughts and doings and

mistakes of a dead woman, will they write in pencil on the margin

– as I found today alongside 'The Burial of Sir John Moore' at 'and

the moonbeams fitful gleaming' –

'Calculated that there could have been no moonlight on the date

of these events.'

(Extract from 'Christabel's Diary' by Marion Angus)

ACKNOWLEDGEMENTS

My thanks go to Marion Angus for dropping a little book of poetry at my feet, for filling my dreams with the 'hints and possibilities' which shape this novel, and for being a great example of tenacity. Also to those in the real world who encouraged me, advised me and helped me to draw *Blackthorn* from my head onto the printed page.

PART I

CHAPTER 1

Corrie Fee, Glen Clova: April 1899

'Tinker' – the word spewed oot like a lump o gristle.

Wull tapped wi a stick, the colour and the twist o the man's face vivid in his mind, the insults ringin in his lugs.

'Be off with you! Guddling fish, snaring rabbits, stealing pheasants… you, you and your kind.'

A rhythm welled up in Wull's heid. He battered at the rock and dammit he was near as guid as Aleckie Gibson, and Aleckie the best drummer he'd ever had in his band. But his drumstick broke. He set the twa bits whaur they'd catch and in the burst o flame squinted aboot – little enough room, but room enough. A surge o heat: woodsmoke tickled his nose.

There wasnae the chance o a snowflake in hell yon bastard o a game-keeper would smell the trout. No, he'd hae his feet up on the mantlepiece, his arse half-wey up the lum and if he wasnae snorin he'd be wonderin why his guid wife had a smile on her face on sic a like nicht.

Wull felt his lip curl and thocht that suited him better than a doff o the cap and a bow o the neck and a beggin o the pardon sir, just passin through, sir. But ach, he'd got his fish oniewey and a bittie oatmeal breid forbye. He thumbed his nose. 'Wull Greig, awa wi ye. Whit if ye did kow-tow? Ye still got the best o it.' His collar set up, he hunkered himsel doon.

Nae moon, nae stars: fire and smoke and mist. He spat in the fire and listened tae the gob sizzle. Time for a stretch... the cheeks o his backside all the better for a rub. At least he'd got tae the cave afore the dark and he'd a stack o wood. His fiddle was in its box, happed against the cauld in a fine wool scarf wi a paisley pattern he'd got frae the widow in Ballater. He wiped a dreep fae his nose wi the back o his hand. Christ he even smellt like a Tinker... and the ither hand as bad. Guid sakes, and him hopin tae see the widow the morn.

Ach, a homely enough smell, and it wouldnae be the first time – nor the last – he'd come tae a lassie frae a campfire.

But God the sleeve o his jaiket stank: the smell o bender tents, campfires, steam fae the big bellied pot – even if whiles it was just just a neep frae the edge o a field that simmered. The shufflin o horses, dogs in amongst feet, tales o trickery and done deals. Somebody would sing, anither play the penny whistle. Sure as the Pole Star Nellie'd hae a story tae tell. Fowk would sit quiet then, bairnies hushed at their mithers' knees, as she spoke o the silkies; how the Broonie tested ye; how Auld Hornie could outwit ye. And how could thae stories hae been passed through the generations if they wasnae true?

At last Wull'd be persuaded... never nae mind for what he'd

play, when he picked the fiddle up, but somebody would aye shout for the tune that was richt. He'd tak it frae there, play strathspeys and marches, reels and slip-jigs, for his cousins and half-cousins on his mither's side, his aunties and uncles – aince removed, twice removed, and whit difference did that mak? He'd play for their joys, their secrets, their loves, their fears and worries. Play till their legs were tired, their feet couldnae tap nae mair, till his fingers were thrawn wi the cauld and the dark gnawed at the embers o the fire.

Quiet, he'd be, as he wrapped his fiddle. Then the logs would settle in a shower o sparks, or an infant would greet, and the spell would be broken. The women would wrap themselves in their shawls and hoist their bairns on their hips, or lead them by the hand: ane then anither, till it was just the men-folk left, the glow o the embers reflected in their faces, the quiet argie-bargie aboot this or that, the wonderment at yon queer wey o daein. The peace micht be broken by a guffaw frae the young lads: nothin mair than that.

There had been a time, that was Wull's wey: the restlessness in his soul, the spring in his step, the need for the wind tae part his hair. But a man could weary o – aye, even just the summer walkin.

The widow now… a man could dae waur. He was richt fond o her, and the thocht o her ham and eggs was enough tae mak him slaver. Nae like the rest, she never looked for nothin. 'I aye think a fiddler has a richt guid rhythm', that was as much as she ever cam awa wi. He shiftit the weight in his breeks. If he got up the road early enough the morn, he'd hae a dook in the loch.

A noise – his heid cocked. He elbow knocked the woodpile.

Sticks shifted and clattered. He lurched tae catch them afore they tumbled ower the cliff, and scarted the flesh on the back o his hand on the thorn bush, bastard thing he'd hae cut back lang ago, but for the fact it kept him awa frae the edge and its moanin was better company than nane on a windy nicht.

The ins and oots o a campfire tale cam intae his heid, gied him the cauld creeps. But Christ, if he was lucky – and when was he no? – whatever it was micht pass him by.

Maybe there was nothin there, but the blade o his knife was aye honed in readiness. His finger and thumb ran its length. He balanced the hilt on his middle finger. Even if that was a cry he heard – and how could he be sure, wi the clatter o the sticks? The blade catched a glint o the fire as it tipped back and forrit. The muscles in his hand, his airm, his hale body stilled. The knife steadied. If there was somethin up there on the moor, what could it be but a wildcat?

'Tyach!' Wull tossed the knife. Catchin the hilt on its wey doon, he slashed at the smoke o the fire. Yon was mair like a beast searchin for a mate than the Earl o Hell aifter a man's supper. He settled himsel back, picked up a branch and whittled the end tae a point. Nae a sound beyond the scrape, the settlin o the fire and the noise in his lugs when he swallowed.

The skin o the trout had started tae shrivel. He poked it. Underneath was pink and moist and – oh my God – the juices that ran in his gullet.

Christ, there it was again.

In his haste tae stand he pressed his palm on a het stane. 'Bastard!' The stane got kicked aside and he tucked the hand intae his oxter. There was a burst o flame. Smoke swirled up roond him and nipped at his een. He leaned his heid back hard against the rock.

'Stupid gowk.' He blew on the sair bit. 'A bloody blister raised already.'

His wits tellt him yon cry was nae spit and hiss o a wildcat, nor the grunt o a deer, nor even the howl o a wolf. But neither was it a ghaist, nor a deil, nor a banshee. Yon was the keenin o flesh and blood: a lost soul. And it was gey close, by Jesus. 'For Christsake!' He cupped baith hands intae a trumpet. 'Wha's there?' His words glanced across the rock. 'Wha's there?' A will-o-the-wisp in his face: his hands flailed. Smoke frae the fire, that was all. Smoke frae the fire. That was it.

Anither cry, and he could mak oot the words this time. 'Is someone there?' His skin like goose flesh that had just been plucked: 'Jesus Christ…'

'Is somebody there?'

'God Almichty, it's a lassie.'

'Help!'

He reached for the trunk o the birk, pulled himsel awa frae the fire. Christ, what was a man tae dae? The ledge was solid enough under his feet, but the path – rough at the best o times, and in the dark – he'd never tried it in the dark – and the mist…

'Help me!'

He saw her in his mind, stumblin tae the comfort o a voice – his voice – and the precipice. 'Bide whaur ye are, for the love o Christ. Bide whaur ye are, lass – dinnae move an inch.' He groped sideways. 'I'll come and get ye.'

'Help me!'

Loose bracken underfoot, that he shoved aside. 'I'll find ye. Never fear, I'll find ye.'

The ledge inched by – nae sae wide at this end, but he groped at the cliff and felt the shift in the angle and then there was the tilt o the path and grit under his fingernails. 'Bide whaur ye are lass, I'm comin.' His feet tested stanes afore he trusted his weight and for a while it was simple enough.

At the first zig-zag o the path he went through the smoke o his ain fire, thanked God for its glimmer and cursed himsel for nae stokin it afore he left. Up again until the path cleaved through rock and he wedged himsel for a minute and leaned his heid back and the face o the cliff rose as far as he could see, though that maybe wasnae far. The blister on his palm had torn so he bit the loose skin aff and put the raw patch tae his open lips.

It was safe here. He'd hae rested langer if there had been the time. But 'I'm comin lass', he shouted, and gied himsel a shove. 'Just bide whaur ye are.'

Nothin back. Standin stock-still: 'Are ye there, lass?'

Nothin. He darenae waste nae mair time.

The path was steeper here. A chill in the air, awa frae the fire, a touch o breeze lettin the mist think it was rain. His hair stuck against his brow. Water was seepin under rock and through rock and dreepin ower rock and his hands was that weet and raw he could hardly feel them, just when he needed them tae be anither pair o een. As much tae himsel as tae the lassie – 'I'm near enough there' – but he'd forgotten yon patch o scree. The feet went frae under him. The boulders were that loose he kent fine they'd shift, it was just how far, that was the worry. Heid first and on his back, a sick feelin in his belly… a heather root, a jolt, airms near torn frae their sockets, a dunt on the heid. And below, the grumble o rocks still on the move.

Black and blue the morn, like enough. But that was better than deid.

A mewl frae up above. She'd heard. Well, thank the Lord at least he kent she was still there. 'I'm still in ae bit,' he shouted.

The path lost now, forget it. But just… up: if he kept clamberin up, ae hand then anither, ae hand then anither.

A surface o thick moss, like fur under his hand, and the smell o smoke frae his fire. If the breeze was comin frae the north… in his mind he fixed the lie o the land and surmised he was near whaur the peat moor hung ower the cliff, a place ye'd keep well awa frae if ye had the option, but if ye didnae ye'd thank yer lucky stars it was that dark ye couldnae see. He spread his weight, tholed the pain in his hand as he clawed at a tangle o heather roots and pulled and hoisted till he got traction wi his elbows. Inch by inch, sideweys, ae leg then the ither, until at last he hauled himsel up and lay flat on his belly in the heather.

He minded tae thank the good Lord and by the time he'd done that he'd enough wind back tae crawl awa frae the edge.

'I'll find ye, now.'

Nae reply. He got tae his feet and peered intae the grey, this wey and that. 'Are ye there? For the love o God, lassie, tell me ye're still there.'

Just the rasp o his ain breith.

'Speak tae me!'

Nae even a whimper.

'I ken ye're there.' But he didnae ken, and if he'd been richt the first time, that would be waur than the cliff path. He calmed himsel and tried again. 'For the love o God, lassie, just tell me whaur ye are.'

Animal fear, he could sniff it in the air, and now he understood a lassie micht wonder what kind o man was oot on a nicht like this. 'Listen. Dinnae worry yersel, lass. I'm nae beast, nor elf, just a mannie on the road, catched in the mist afore I got doon the track. A bit like yersel.'

'Over here.'

His heid swivelled tae the sound.

'I'm over here.' A pause. 'I don't... I'm... I can't tell you more than that.'

'Fair enough.' Wull was turnin tae the sound o her: 'Just haud the grip lass, for a wee while. Dinnae get yersel in a fankle.' If he couldnae trust his een, a man had ither senses. He planted himsel and breithed the mist deep intae his lungs and tensed, like a cat on the prowl. 'Can ye keep speakin tae me... or just clap yer hands, lass.' His ear picked up the thud o leather on leather. 'There now, I hae ye. Keep daein that.'

'It's this way. I'm over here. But I can't see a thing. I don't know which way I'm facing.'

The peatbog sucked at Wull's boots. He minded the great granite boulder. That was whaur a bodie would stop, get their back against that. His voice sure now: 'Hang in there lass, ye'll be at the stane? I'm near enough there.' He heard a sniff and kent he was richt and maybe a wee greet wouldnae dae her nae harm. 'Bide whaur ye are lass.' He edged forward and thank Christ, there it was, the shape o the boulder. A man's feet were surer when he'd somethin tae aim for. 'I've near as dammit got ye.'

'I see you! I see you!' Ae arm waved, the ither kept its arch tae the stane. 'Over here, this way!'

Like a wraith she looked, but there was a hert thumpin in the body that clung tae him and rested its heid against his neck. A taller body than he'd had in his mind, though skinny – nae an ounce o spare flesh – and thirty if she was a day. Dressed the wey toffs dress for the hills – a lang skirt and a jaiket that covered her backside, a waistcoat and tie like a man's and a silly-like hat. But ye couldnae fault her boots.

She pulled awa that sudden Wull took a step back and wiped his hands on his breeks, though they were caked wi glaur and he near cried oot wi the pain. 'Sorry miss, for the gutters.'

She crossed her airms ower her chest. 'No, no, don't worry, it's not that. Just, I'm sorry. Look, I'm not usually…'

Wull put on the voice that would let her ken she'd be safe and that he could deal wi the likes o her and it wouldnae put him up nor doon. 'Richt, now. Whaur was the ither… was there some mair o yer party, lass? On the hill wi ye?'

It could hae been a shak or a nod or maybe she just didnae understand. 'Did ye lose yer freinds?'

She gied a wave that tellt him nothin.

'Ye were oot wi yer freinds?'

'A friend.'

'And whaur did ye lose her? What happened?'

'He left.'

'Left?'

'Yes, but that was before the mist came down.'

'Left ye by yersel?'

'No. Well, yes, but not like that. He didn't leave me. It was me. I wanted to walk on my own.'

'In the mist?'

'Look, it wasn't like that. I told you. There was no sign of mist then. And I'm quite capable. I'm used to the hills you know. I walk a lot. Just, it came down so quickly. One minute, and… I did look for shelter, but it was hopeless by then.'

It was nane o his business, and a relief he didnae hae tae look for somebody else. 'Yer teeth are chitterin.'

'I didn't expect, you know, when I shouted… I didn't think anyone would hear.'

The voice posh, but nae airs and graces. 'Gied me a richt fleg.'

'Sorry.'

'No, no, I dinnae mean nothin.'

'At least there are two of us lost now.'

'I'm nae lost.'

'You know how to get us off the hill?'

'Aye, but haud yer horses, in the mornin.'

'It can't be far though, surely. To the glen road?'

'And whit glen would that be, miss?' Christ, she didnae like that… he put his good palm up. 'Look, I didnae mean tae be cheeky.'

'Can we at least try? I'm wet through. I'll freeze to death.'

'Havers. Nae wi a fine tweed jaiket like that. This is nae mair than a smirny rain noo that'll clear by the dawn. And it's near enough the end o April. Dinnae worry, lass, I'll look aifter ye. I've a wee fire – and I must hae kent ye were comin, for I kept a bittie trout for yer supper.'

'You've food? And a fire?'

Her hair was cut close intae the nape o her neck. 'And a shelter forbye, a place tae rest yer heid, if ye're nae that fussy. Are ye comin?'

'Is it far?'

'Nae that far. I'll lead ye.'

'In the dark?'

'Look lass, I'm nae bidin up here aw nicht. And I'm nae gaein doon nae glen. Ye can follow me if ye want and if ye dinnae, well, ye'll likely hae yer reasons. I'll nae force ye. But I'm gaein back tae my wee fire and my bed tae pass the nicht and if ye want tae come wi me, ye're mair than welcome.'

'I'll come. Of course I will. Thank you. I didn't mean to offend. I'm just anxious, I suppose. A little shocked.'

'Aye, but there's just ae thing. Ye dinnae sleepwalk, dae ye?'

'No.'

'That's damned lucky.'

∽

'That wey. In there.' He pushed her intae the cave wi the flat o his guid hand against her back. 'Ye've done it. Ye'll be fine now, just get yersel sorted.' It must hae been a harder push than he meant for her feet shuffled on the bracken and she stumbled.

But nae hairm done. He turned his back and let his breith oot slow – quiet so she wouldnae hear – and waited for his hert tae calm doon.

'Can I have… I'll need my skirt back.'

He could hae spared her that reid face. 'Aye', he said. 'Ye will that, lass. Sorry.'

'You were quite right. It was an encumbrance.'

'Here, tak it – anither fine bit tweed, though maybe nae as fine as it was this mornin. Just mind and nae trip ower it again, or ye micht brak yer neck next time.'

'I still don't know how you managed to catch me. I thought that was really it. You saved my life.'

'Aye, well, that's as may be. We'll nae dwell on it.' He gied himsel a shak. He didnae ken either – would never ken – how he'd managed. It must hae been meant, that was the only thing. 'Just get in there, lass and sort yersel.' And if she got that torn skirt ower her arse, the wey she'd been jitterin, that'd be anither miracle. 'Listen, I've just minded. There's a bittie sack in the back. Put that ower yer shoulders.'

'You're very kind.'

Her voice was muffled: her back tae him. Wull leaned ower the embers and hoped he could get it tae catch, though he was hindered by the hand that wouldnae grip. That wee bit stick micht be enough, though, if he could…

A rustle frae ahent: 'There. That'll do. But I can hardly see. I can't find the sack.'

'It's on the flair, lassie, just grope for it. Or maybe ye dinnae ken whit a sack feels like?'

Shuffling noises. 'I've got it.'

Nae offence taen, thank Christ. Wi a bit o luck she hadnae even heard him. Bark touched against the twig: a spark, a curl o smoke. He set the tinder doon and laid a couple o sticks across. 'And we're in luck. The fire's catched. Twa ticks and ye'll feel the heat and see as much as ye need tae see.'

'I don't know how I'll ever be able to thank you.'

Mair smoke. He blew again, concentrated. Fires needed coaxed, and he was guid at that. He'd been settin fires since he was a lad, that'd been his job, back in the cottar hoose. He minded the wee wooden stool – the ane his faither made – hard up against the fender, the heat on his face and the draught on his back, the hiss and spit o cheap coal, the kettle swingin on its chain, the smell o mutton fat candles and the rustle o the chaff when Cissy crawled intae the box bed wi the wee anes.

He balanced twigs against ane anither. The flames licked, and climbed higher. Sittin back on his heels, Wull watched his wee fire draw in air tae feed itsel and listened tae its crackle, and oh the satisfaction, the pleasure in a heat that could roast a rabbit on a spit and gie licht enough tae show the flesh part frae the bone as ye tore at the haunch.

'You're very patient.'

The sack was folded across her chest like a plaid. Gey awkward – gawky even – she stood, though her face was handsome enough, now he'd a richt deek – a dome o a foreheid.

Her hands stretched tae the flames. 'I don't know how to thank you. I don't know what to say.'

'Dinnae say nothin then. Just for God's sake keep that bloody skirt awa frae the fire, or ye'll burn like a witch. He glanced up, shamefaced. 'Sorry for the language, miss.'

She pulled the hem in aboot. 'It's all right. I'll be careful. I didn't want to die up there and I don't now.'

'Ye'll be fine. Sit yersel doon.'

'Up there on the moor I remembered a dream I had – not so long ago. I was in a garden. There was thick mist and everything – trees, walls, flowers, grass – everything was a shade of grey. I searched and searched for colour – any colour would have made me happy. I walked round and round, trying to find a way out, trying to see over the walls, but they were too high and there were no gates. I began to panic – in the dream. Everything seemed so hopeless, so bleak, and there was nothing I could do about it. At the thought of, you know – not being able to… to do anything! I believe I would've suffocated to death, if I hadn't managed to waken up.'

Her lips moved the wey a teacher's did when they were tellin you somethin they thocht ye should ken.

'It was like that, up there.'

Gie the wifie her due, she must hae had a richt fleg. And that was some sair tumble she took and here she was and not a girn. Wull gripped his left hand roond his richt wrist and tried tae straighten the fingers. The burnt flesh yarked. 'Aye, lass, but ye must hae hurt yersel when ye fell?'

She gied her elbow a rub. 'No, not really. Nothing broken anyway!'

'Sit yersel doon at the fire, lass.'

She hunkered doon, stared at the flames. Wull cleared a flat stane o debris and set his water can tae boil. He cut a doorstepper frae the breid, held it tae the fire on a stick. The flesh o the fish had dried and shrunk. 'It'll be gey...' he held it tae his nose. 'Aye, smoked. And mind for the wee banes.'

Her fingers still clumsy wi the cauld. 'But what about you?'

'I've had mine. Get it doon ye.' He couldnae help but see the wey she held her airm and hand.

'Are you sure?' But she didnae pause in the eatin o it. 'I didnae realise how hungry I was. I didnae even think aboot food.'

'I'll mak a cuppie tea.' Wull was watchin the bubbles rise in his can when he realised whit she'd just said. He unwrapped the paper poke and threw a puckle leaves in.

'Will ye let it mash?'

He gied himsel a minute or twa. 'Ye mean infuse, dae ye no?'

A wee smile: 'Aye,' she said. ' "infuse" is guid enough if ye like yer tea peelywally.'

'Ye want yer tea black?'

'Aye.'

'Lucky again. I dinnae hae nae milk.'

She was pickin at the skeleton o the fish. 'Oh, that was so good! Thank you God!' Lookin up tae whaur the stars should be, there was somethin like a bairn aboot her. 'I'm so grateful' – a wee break in her voice, the first, and she got ower it gey quick. 'But if it hadnae been for you...'

'That's just the wey luck gaes, bad, then it turns. It aye turns.' It was guid tae see how she savoured the crumbs.

'They say that if you save somebody's life, you're responsible for that person – for the rest o their life.'

'That's my luck then.'

'I'd never hae found this cave.'

'Naw.'

'Did you find it by yoursel?' Christ, there she was lickin her fingers.

'Naw.'

'Did someone… somebody bring you here?'

'Aye.'

'Anither Tinker?'

He broke a stick and set the twa bits each side o the tea can.

'You are a Tinker, aren't you?'

His hands still busy: 'And if I was?'

'Oh, I didn't mean… please don't think – it's just, well, there was a Tinker woman I knew. I kent. She camped in the woods near Arbroath, every summer. Sold clothes pegs, chrysanthemums. Told fortunes, that kind o thing. Nellie. I was really fond o Nellie. I just wondered if… maybe you knew her?'

Nellie would hae thocht the brew was a fine colour.

'Sometimes when she spoke… and her stories.'

Wull kept his heid doon.

'And her words, like poetry, almost. Without trying. And her voice, it came through her somehow, from somewhere else.'

The conyach[1] in it, aye in his ears.

Somebody has tae dae it laddie. Somebody has tae walk the land.

Nae for the smell o wild garlic, the bloom o the heather. Nae for the first bonnie bank o snaw. Nae for nuthin but that the land cries oot for the tread o feet the wey a lassie wants her skin touched.

---

1. Spirit.

But God help ye, son, if ye've heard her cry. She's a wild mistress, the land.

He'd heeded the cry, had he nae? He'd left his hame and walked the tracks, and if life was hard he hardened wi it. Sometimes the land lent him power – strength frae the summit ridge. Whiles he drank comfort frae a burn. Sometimes paths hurried by under his feet and found him shelter or a clump o blaeberries or a kestrel's nest wi fower eggs. The land kent the tramp o his feet the wey his fiddle kent the rhythm o his fingers. But ae thing he'd learned – he gied the tea a stir and tapped the stick on the edge o the can – Tinkers and country folk, there were guid and bad and every shade in atween. Folk, were folk, were folk – loyal tae their ain afore the likes o him: a blue buck[2] born and a blue buck till he deid.

'Painted pictures wi her words, that's what Nellie did.'

He thrust the tea can at her. 'Here, tak it.' Christ, what was he thinkin, and he hadnae even asked her name. 'I've camped here since I was a laddie.'

'A fine shelter.'

'Guid enough for the last wolf ever seen in Scotland.'

'Really!' She held the can so as nae tae burn hersel. 'This is good, just how Nellie used tae mak tea.'

'She gied ye tea?'

'Oh aye! I kent Nellie from when I was – what fourteen maybe? I used to get awa frae the house, when I could. I'd been ill, you see, and… it was a bad epidemic. Lots of people died… I was one of the lucky ones, but the disease damaged my heart and

2. A person of mixed parentage i.e. only one Traveller parent.

when I began tae get better the doctor said I'd to… I'd tae get as much fresh air as I could, and exercise. So my parents just… well, I'd a lot of freedom actually, more than most… maist o my friends.'

The tea can was passed across. She was genuine, that was clear. He'd speak tae her aboot Nellie, but nae yet. First things first: he'd better get her settled, for it was just kindlin he'd left, and it wouldnae last the nicht.

'I used tae meet Nellie in the woods – she was somebody I could talk tae. It was when you said you'd a place tae sleep, I wondered then if…'

'Ye'll nae mind sharin yer bed wi a Tinker man, then?'

By God, she looked younger then and feisty, a spark in her. 'No, it's all right. I mean, I wouldnae dream o takin your bed.'

'Just a wee joke, lass. Ye'll hae seen yersel, it's nae muckle o a bed, but ye're welcome tae what bracken there is.' He lit a cigarette frae the fire.

She stared straight aheid. 'No, I really couldnae tak… but… I dinnae suppose… I wouldn't mind…' wavin a hand at his fag: 'Could you spare one?'

'You smoke?'

'Just one o my bad habits.'

He held open the packet, offered it to her. She steadied his hand to light her cigarette. They both drew heavily and deeply. Wull poked the fire and added sticks.

'You know… there's something else I'm wondering about. I don't – dinnae – mean tae pry, but… may I ask you somethin?

Wull shrugged.

'In the cave, under the sack. Was that a violin case?'

'Could be.'

'You play?'

'I micht.'

'Well, actually, I'm wondering… it's strange isn't it, I can hardly credit it, but I think I might even know who you are.'

'You hae the advantage, miss.'

'The name's Marion. Marion Angus.'

He inclined his heid.

'I'm from Arbroath. And if I'm right, I ken your sister. You have a sister?'

'Mair than ane.'

'Cissy? Cissy Greig? Is Cissy your sister? She was at school wi me. We were friends.'

'You and Cissy?'

'A long time ago, now.'

'Wait a meenit… your faither'll be the minister, then?'

'That's it! Your mother's funeral. That's when I saw you. Wull, isn't it?'

'Hae ye seen Cissy?'

'We lost touch.' She pulled the bittie sack tichter roond her shoulders.

Wull roused himsel and said she must be fair done, and it wasnae gettin nae warmer. She should try and sleep, for they'd start at the dawnin. In the shelter he scraped the bracken thegither tae mak a cushion. She sat on that, her back against the rock.

He heard her shift and stretch and shift again and after a

whilie she said would he nae just come in, for she could see the fire gaein doon and there was room enough and she was worried sick he'd catch his deith o cauld, for how would she get back up that cliff by hersel?

'Ah weel,' he said, 'you've somethin there' and squeezed in and the only wey his airm would fit was roond her back and across her shoulder. He didnae think she was sleepin, but there was nothin mair said and that was a relief.

He dreamed o a lassie dancin: clockwise and back, clockwise and back, her feet beatin a pattern on bare red clay.

The fire was deid when he wakened, chilled tae the bone and wi an empty belly. There was nae colour but the black o the nicht. The only thing tae dae was snuggle up and let her heid rest on his breist and her hair tickle his cheek. His hand – across her chest – rose and fell, rose and fell. He tried tae think aboot the morn, but the smell o her... she cuddled in and said somethin but though he strained his lugs he couldnae mak it oot. The sack had slipped so he happed her up again and willed the heat in his body tae warm her hert. And this time, as he dozed, it was her, he kent it was her, even in the dream he kent it was her in the water. She floated in a river, pulled further and further awa by the current, her skin that white she micht hae been a reflection o the bonnie silver moon. But his fear was less than his wonderment – not a splash nor a ripple nor a wave did she mak, just let hersel drift.

He wouldnae sleep again.

First licht, the moon white, the mist rollin back: her weight still against him. Her mop o hair, short, fine and frizzy, and he'd aye liked a lassie wi a lang thick heid o hair she could let doon. But there was somethin aboot that neck – thin and lang like the neck o his fiddle, but sturdy enough for the heid that sat on it: the skin o her cheek smooth under his fingers. He could only shak his heid at the screive and the swellin on her wrist and wish he'd a root o comfrey.

A very comely curve tae her bosom, and it was high time he made a move. Her airm heavy, but easy lifted, he slipped frae underneath and hoped she'd sleep on a while.

A current o air flurried the ashes o the fire. The rays o the sun were crestin the horizon. In the glen, mist still lay in the hollows, thicker at the Linn. Clumps o woodland poked through banks o silver grey. He heard her stir and felt his blood quicken.

Lay doon yer heid upon my knee

He didnae ken why he was singin. She came up ahent him.

'I like that ballad. It's one of my favourites.'

The wey she looked, sleep in her een, face white and peakit and dirty, claes muddy and crumpled and torn… and nae a trace o shyness or discontent.

And see ye not that bonnie road
That winds aboot the faerie brae?
That is the road tae fair elfland
Whaur you and I this nicht maun gae.

Her singin voice was timid, but mind, yon wasnae a song ye'd expect a wifie like her tae ken. 'Christ lassie, look at the state o ye. Ye could be a Tinker wife yersel!'

A cock cried far below, as clear and sharp as if they were up tae their ankles in the muck o the fairmyaird. Wull felt shame-faced then, though there was nae reason for it. The twa o them stood side by side and looked beyond the corries, across the scree and the bracken covered slopes tae the glen that was mair and mair exposed by the liftin o the mist: the fields, the woods, the faerie knolls, the river that twisted and plunged its wey tae Strathmore.

Wull's een took in the tracks: the patterns his ancestors had marked on the land.

'What literature, what poetry, what art could do this justice?'

The Bard hadnae done bad, he minded that, but somethin in her words – he couldnae put a finger on it – raivelled him. Riled him, by God. Did she think he'd never... him and his fiddle, they could dae it justice, that's whit. Ower the years his fiddle had picked up echoes o the islands, o straths and glens, lochs and rivers, moors, passes, the great peaks. If he wanted, he could play the tunes o his country for a month and never repeat himsel.

Ach, but she'd never hae time for the likes o him, there was nae sense in it. Posh, she was, had never wanted for nothin. She'd been speakin the Scots last nicht just tae humour him, nothin else, and he couldnae be daein wi fowk like that.

As if she'd heard his thochts: 'Aye, the licht. This time o day... nae much can beat that.'

They heard a noise and looked up. A pair o golden eagles,

wings heavy in the still air. She put her neck richt back tae follow their upward spiral. A whisper: 'Can ye hear it Wull?' Her hand rested on his shoulder. 'Can ye?'

It was surely his hunger kept his mooth shut.

'The music.'

'They soar the better on a strong wind,' he managed tae get oot. Wi his knife he scarted lichen frae the bark o the wee birk, but there she was again at his back.

'How can it grow, Wull, that tree, frae that teeny crack in the rock?'

He turned sharp. Blue her een, or was that a shade o grey? And oh my God, there was a fleck in them, just like his mither had.

She traced the trunk wi a finger, tae whaur the rock had split.

'Gey lang roots, if ye ask me.'

'And that bush – the blackthorn. How can it flourish here? Look at these buds.'

It was the dew on them catchin the early sun.

'Such ticht, ticht buds,' she said, 'the slightest tinge o green on white.' Her hand made a wee circle above the bush, then anither and anither.

'What is it?'

'A bit o the windin sheet o Mary, that unravelled as she ascended tae heaven.' She held up a strand o gossamer.

Wull couldnae help but laugh. 'Nellie?'

'Nellie.'

'Yer faither'll nae like that idea much.'

'Blossom on the blackthorn, blossom on blackthorn.'

'They'll burst the day, wi that sun.'

'Pearls, that's what they're like. Pearls on blackthorn. Seed pearls.'

'Dinnae touch! Watch yersel, and mind that branch, it'll rip ye tae bits.' He pulled her back. 'A black hert, it has, yon bush.'

'Oh, but I don't mind. It's so beautiful today.'

'We'd best be gettin on the road.'

'I wish I could bide a while.'

'That's the water gone, and the sticks, and there'll be folk oot lookin for ye.'

'Maybe I could come back.'

'It's nae private.'

'It was almost worth gettin lost.'

'Ye werenae that far aff the path.'

'The truth is… I was lost afore the mist came doon.'

Wull held his coonsel.

'Mama always – aye says, if there's a richt and a wrong path, I'll tak the wrong one.'

'There's nae sic a thing as a wrong path.'

'I've found a few.'

'It's nae whaur ye've been, it's whaur ye gae that matters. Did Nellie never tell ye? A man follaes his ain road, he'll get whaur he's meant tae be.'

CHAPTER 2

Arbroath: May 1899

The shadow o the shed pointed richt at his taes. Ach, but whit wi the bend in the road and the bushes... he kent how tae blend intae a background. As well it was a bonnie mornin, and as well he was a patient man, for that was the third quarter the kirk clock had struck since he settled himsel, and there was nae sign o life yet, bar somebody that shook a duster frae an upstairs windae, and an auld man on his knees, tiein up tulips in the next-door gairden.

His pocket watch said the same: she was later the day than yesterday. But a quiet determination, that's whit he had tae see this through. And by God, his chin was smooth. There was nothin like sittin in a barber's chair – the sting o the razor – tae mak ye see straicht. And though he was sayin it himsel, the man had done wonders wi the scissors, and that wee touch o brilliantine.

The gairdens full o the colours o spring: Dalhousie Place, the sign said. He minded when he was a young lad he'd stabled the Earl's horse – a big beast, a chestnut – and didnae get a whit for his trouble. Aye, the Dalhousies, the Erskines, the Ogilvies, the lot o them: built dykes across the land tae match lines drawn on maps by bigwigs in Edinburgh – or London – as if that could mak it their land.

The door she was ahent had fancy stained gless and there was somethin movin there but he forced himsel tae haud back. Rash and reckless he would not be, nae the day. Yon blue jaiket, and the same wee sailor hat: it was her. She hesitated in the porch, turned back, spoke tae somebody in the lobby. Half-wey doon the gairden, she stopped for some words wi the gairdener. A hearty laugh and cheerie-bye.

Let her get distance frae the hoose: nae need tae push his luck.

She followed the contour, awa frae the toon, and whaur the last o the hooses gied wey tae a copse o trees, cut though a path ye'd hardly hae kent was there. Swallows skimmed the surface o the burn. Further doon the hill a wagon wi empty ale-casks clattered doon the slope, splashed through the water. Twa drey horses, knee deep, drank their fill.

She plucked stems o marsh marigold, twirled them under her nose. On the wee wooden brig every flooer was cast on the water. Watchin the patterns drift doonstream, she'd the look o a body mesemerised.

This wasnae the place.

Some thocht must hae gien her a kick up the backside. Gaein through the back streets – busy this time o day wi workin folk – she kept up a pace, then up her skirts aboon her ankles and near ran alang the path that came oot at the Ladybridge. The stink o tanneries catched at the back o Wull's throat, made him cough up phlegm and hacker in the cundie.

It was the High Street she turned ontae, but there was nae sign o her when he got there. The bell on the tea-shop jangled. He sneaked a look in the windae and there she was, leanin ower a table tae poke at the crust o a pastry tart wi a fork. But it was just another lass she was wi. He'd hae liked tae be in her pooch. But this was neither the time nor the place.

Half an hour, and the twa women were back on the pavement, Miss Marion wi a poke in her hand. The ither lass pecked a kiss on her cheek and hurried awa.

A forward lean tae her as she turned shorewards. Just the twa stops: on the railway brig, tae keek at the express as it gaed by, and at the corner o Shore Road when she spoke tae the rag and bone man. Some urchins liftin boulders alow the tide mark shouted her tae come and look, but she just waved wi ae hand and held ontae her hat wi the ither, though there was nae breeze tae speak o. It was the links again, that's whaur she was gaein. He looked across the water tae Fife Ness and the Isle o May, the castle and cathedral ruins o St Andrews.

The sparrows were waitin. They rose half-wey tae catch the crumbs she scattered, pecked at her feet amongst the buttercups when the poke was empty.

Whaur the beach started, she settled hersel on the grass, feet on the sand. Wull stopped ahent a bank o whin, in twa minds. It was just... afore he spoke, he'd need tae be clear, hae his mind made up, whit it was he was askin o her.

Caw cannie, Wull lad.

He paced back and fore, as far as the whin would hide him. Dinnae lay it on ower thick... cajole her. He could dae that. Aye, maybe, if he kept his wits, but the like o her – she wasnae daft, she could wipe the flair wi him if she wanted. For the love o God, man, if ye get it wrang ye'll maybe never get anither chance.

What if he just came oot wi it?

Wi what?

A quick check o the beach and back and fore he went again.

He could dae the banter: that was the wit o a man. Aye, self-praise nae recommendation, but he'd a pawkiness women liked. Nothin vulgar. A man o few words, usually. Didnae waste his breith – saved it tae cool his porridge like his mither had aye tellt him tae. But Miss Marion micht nae like that, wi her education... and maybe he was gruff, some hae said as much, ower the years.

Och, but times there was nae words for the things a man wanted tae say, and there was some words he'd never... didnae suit him, nae the wey he was.

It was quiet here. Just the waves, that was whit he heard. Nae loud – a murmur – but it was funny how a noise like that crept under a man's skin. The sound o the waves, like the breeze through... damn it! Whit the hell was wrang? He could hardly fathom it. He hadnae lost sleep ower a lassie, nae since he was a young lad in a field o grass and in the early weeks o summer that was surely the bonniest place in the world: the whisper o the breeze and the smell o the earth and… the shock. The stirring, the rush and the surge o blood, the wey he couldnae think straicht – thoughts in his heid like a tangled skein o wool, and he understood now how that had got his faither in sic a rage. The wey the lassie just cam oot wi it: 'I love you, Wull Greig,' as if she wasnae Miss Violet Augusta Mary Frederica Kennedy-Erskine hersel: as if he wasnae just Wull Greig frae the cottar hooses, as if it was just a simple thing tae say.

He'd never wanted that kind o aggravation again. Oh, he'd nuzzle intae the flesh ahent a lassie's neck, he'd dae that, they liked that. That said as much as a puckle words… and sometimes got ye intae as much trouble.

Gulls were awkward bloody things on the sand, heavy, but in flight… Christ, they made it look easy.

She'd her wee notebook oot again, surely wasnae in nae hurry tae gae hame.

If he didnae stop this back and fore he'd wear his tackity boots oot… aye, he could keep her in sicht if he leaned on yon stump. He settled back and drew the salt air intae his gut, let his mind roam free, waited for the wisdom o the earth tae seep through the soles o his feet: for the land tae speak.

Christ, it wouldnae even gie him the time o day, and likely enough neither would she.

The early bummer went. Wull's een were drawn back tae the toon. Even frae here ye could smell the lums o the mills, aye spewin oot their dirt. There was nae wey o kennin for sure if that was the end o Cissy's shift, but some guid micht come o this palaver yet. It'd mak sense, when he was here, tae see Cissy. It would likely please Miss Marion tae hear he'd made his peace wi her.

But her nose was still stuck in the book, and dammit whit was he thinkin? She micht nae even recognise him if he stood next tae her in the queue for a Wattie's bridie.

A puppy hurled itsel at his legs, the tail waggin the backside. He clapped it on the heid. A man reekin o baccy smoke catched up.

If she heard voices she'd maybe look ower, but he couldnae check, nae wi the puppy runnin circles roond him. 'Nae a bad lookin bitch.'

The man stood ready for a blether. 'Nae a bad day either. Mak the maist o it, son.'

Wull gied a thumbs up.

'Ye'll be a stranger?'

'Nae tae ma freinds.' The mein o his face cancelled oot offence.

The puppy hunkered doon, then made a run for the longer grass. 'Christ, she's aifter a rabbit.' A wave, and he was awa.

Wull made as if tae walk back, but stopped at the end o the whin bushes. Miss Marion was rubbin the beast's ears. Natural, the wey she'd a word or twa wi the mannie and dusted the sand aff hersel.

She was gaein hame. This was the place and this was the time: the twa o them on the same track, gaein in different directions. He'd walk on, keep his heid doon and just as they were passin he'd lift his bonnet and act dumfoonered and say 'God's sake, is it you Miss Marion? Fancy meetin you here.'

It'd gie her a turn, but she'd surely recognise him then and she'd say 'Wull Greig! I've been hoping to meet you again.' Well, maybe nae the last bit, but maybe aye, because that was the kind o thing polite folk said, even if they didnae mean it.

He'd pray she was nane the worse for her trouble on the hills, and could he enquire how her airm had healed?

She'd wonder what he was daein in Arbroath, but he was ready for that. It was for business, he'd say – some work for the band – nae fib if he could sort something oot. She'd likely ask for Cissy but he'd tell her he'd just arrived and Cissy would be workin so he thocht he'd hae a wander tae the beach till the evenin.

That made sense.

She'd maybe link her airm in his, the wey she'd done when they came aff the hill, and he'd say it'd be his pleasure tae walk her back tae the toon, and – this a new idea – could she by any chance suggest a teashop?

Christ almighty, she was awa in the opposite direction, and there was not a bit o cover on the beach.

What was waur? Tae run aifter her, or lose her? He couldnae mak up his mind, so just stood whaur he was, shook his heid at his bad luck and mouthed thae curses he couldnae say oot loud.

Hardly mair than a speck, she was, when she left the beach, zig-zagged through a patch o rushes and cut across the corner o a field. Wull narrowed his eeen against the sun and read the land. If it was a path she was on – must be – it'd bring her... he was good at this, he'd work it oot. The high road ran by yon woodie on the shoulder o the hill, and that'd tak her back hame.

If he was tae sneak up by the burn he could cut richt across the links and catch her up there.

Dappled shade in the den, and that suited him better than the beach. Shoots o fern rumpled through the broon husks o last year. Nuthin moved but a faimily o rabbits warmin their noses on a bank, puddocks teemin in a pool, a ferret that scuttled across Wull's path and her steppin oot like she was leadin him in a dance.

She perched hersel on a low-slung branch o beech and stared at the Grampians in the distance. Wull jooked ahent a thicket that sheltered the spot. Runnin water... a grand place for a camp.

Nellie. This was Nellie's camp.

It shamed him, this lurkin ahent trees, and her lookin that content wi hersel. Christ, the conceit o him, makin the hale thing up. The back o his heid clunked against the tree. There was nothin, nothin aboot the wey she looked, nothin aboot the wey she stood – square shouldered, face tipped up – tae say she'd be interested in the likes o him.

A lingerin note, the bell o the kirk strikin one, set aff a melody in Wull's heid. He couldnae place it, though somewey or ither – G major, 3/4 time – it put him in mind o a Neil Gow lament.

The crack o a branch and she was on her feet and whit she'd spied was a laburnum that must hae seeded itsel. Like a tree, she was, drippin blossom, airms that fu she could hardly see her wey aheid as she stepped oot on the road hame.

Ach, there must be better things for a man tae dae wi his time. Whit's mair, surely, the wey she walked, she'd flat feet.

~

He was all the better for the ale at the Volunteer Arms, and the easy company o the country lads that made room for him at the bar but didnae press for conversation.

He'd expected the rough side o Cissy's tongue, but bar a few hame truths she seemed glad enough tae see him. Whether it was ower this thing or that, he'd never been sure, maybe even went back tae him leavin hame, but for his part he'd aye had a saft spot for his wee sister.

But at the mention o Miss Marion! Christ! It ill became Cissy, that scowl. If she'd just came oot wi it, whitever it was, that would hae been somethin. But she'd damned Miss Marion wi the curl o her lip… that took him aback.

It was likely enough just somethin in Cissy's heid, some slight she'd taen ower nothin. The plain fact was, the whats and whyfores never had made nae difference tae Cissy. Black and white, she saw things.

And Miss Marion had been that gracious, not a bad word had she said aboot Cissy. That was the measure o her. And he had seen somethin in her een, he had.

It was the een gied ye awa, every time.

CHAPTER 3

Lunan Bay: July, 1899

The melody was sweet in his heid, and as well as that there was the smell o the meadow, the slant o sun, dew drops on the grass – bronze and gold and silver and grey grass, broon and yellow grass, every stem tipped wi life burstin through. A clover at hand, and he sucked the heid o it, drifted in the hum o bees, the distant sang o a lark. Twa craws skraiked, swooped and flapped at a buzzard.

Shouted words: a guffaw, laughter, back and fore frae folk that were on the road already.

Wull sat up. His fingers worried at his lucky penny – a young queen wi a bun on it, though she didnae look nothin like that noo. The copper brassy against his lips: he flicked the penny, catched it on the back o his hand.

Heids it was, and a grand day for the beach.

A blind man could hae found his wey by the tramp o feet, by the chatter, the yells and whoops, by the crunch o hooves and

wheels on gravel, by the barkin o farm dogs that didnae ken sic
bustle was tae be expected on a holiday. Near every five minutes,
them treadin the road made wey for a cairt or a carriage, sized
up the horses as they passed. Wifies checked the state o their
ankles, bairns shouted cheek and got a clip on the lug for it.
Three men catched up wi Wull and asked whaur he'd left his
fiddle? Their stride matched his, so the fower o them traivelled
the road thegither, tearin tae bits the damp squib that had been
the boxin match in the public hall the nicht afore. Ane swore it
had been rigged, and there micht he been an argie-bargie, but
the further they got frae Arbroath, the mair their minds turned
tae the fear that the fish at Ethiehaven would be flegged awa by
the boats. And hech, it was ower bonnie a day.

The gaggle o folk split when some took the track for Ethiehaven: further on again, for Corbie Knowe. Mill-lassies on the
back o a works cairt chortled and trailed the ends o their shawls
for Wull. He took a breather – a lean against a wild gean –
smoked a fag and watched them trundle doon the road.

On again, through the sweep o the fields: the flattened curve
o the bay aheid, ruins on a hummock o a hill. The castle: she'd
mentioned the castle.

Grey belches against blue – an engine driver lettin aff steam –
and everybody looked the same wey, at a train on the line. A
pony bristled, reared, set aff at a canter. Wull sprinted, catched
the bridle: held firm as the pony shivered.

The faither o the young lad on its back huffed up, offered his
hand. 'Thank ye kindly, sir. I see ye've a wey wi the horses.'

The beast calmed as Wull stroked its neck.

'Bloody nuisance, that station,' the man said. 'Bloody noise and bloody dirt and things are nae the wey they uised tae be. Half the folk in the bloody country will be at Lunan the day.'

By God, and that's how she'd get there, on the train. He should hae thocht o that.

'Ye wouldnae need tae lose somebody on the sands. Ye'd never find them.'

There was a crush o folk ahent, mair comin doon the road aheid and that micht just be a blue jaiket. 'Ye would not.' Wull handed the reins back tae the young lad.

'We've come frae Friockheim,' the man said. 'Hae ye come far yersel?

The blue jaiket was lost in the crowd.

'I have that.' Wull tipped his bonnet and took his leave o the man and his laddie and the road. He followed the flow o folk on a path through the trees, aye scannin for a face or a glimpse o hair cut blunt against a neck, his ears aye cocked for a voice wi a low pitch, for a tongue that didnae prattle. Up high at the castle, he looked back across a land swathed in green – the early shoots o the year's harvest, the links o Lunan, ruffled and folded, studded wi swathes o reed beds and whin, tussocks o couch grass, lyme grass and marram. At the edge o the cliff he looked doon on the Lunan Water that sneaked frae the reeds, cut the beach in half, and drew a line o white spume whaur it pushed against the tide.

Wull shaded his een against the glare o the sea that shimmered wi licht and reflected the blue o the sky. Just a few clouds, banked on the horizon. A foreign rigged schooner moored in the bay was jostled by barques, fishin boats, rowin boats, punts. Beyond the beach, tae the south, was a rocky shore, cliffs, and a wee harbour he took tae be Ethiehaven: north, cliffs crumbled intae the sea.

The castle ruins were battered and scourged by men and time and winds and green algae. His fingers probed the grain o the sandstane, the dimples, the honeycombs. He traced the curves o harder veins.

She wasnae there.

He pulled the sea air intae his lungs.

'My sisters… some friends,' was whit she'd said. 'A picnic.'

'Aye?' he'd said, and she'd waited for him tae ask the questions that were there, on the tip o his tongue though his lips wouldnae let them through. He'd stared up at the tree canopy and she'd taen an age tae pick a threid aff her jaiket.

Well, he'd find her. He strode oot for Ethiehaven, against the flow: the banter o folk aff boats. When he got tae the harbour the men he'd walked wi hailed him. 'Sadies, look at the beauties.'

'A rare supper, that, poached in vinegar water.'

They offered him a line, but he held up the flat o his hand.

'Nae need tae be lanesome on the holiday.'

'Nae fear,' Wull said.

'Ah, ye're meetin somebody, sir?'

'Micht be that.'

'A lassie?' The three o them cheered and said he was a dark horse, he'd kept gey quiet aboot that.

The turn o the tide brocht a breeze and on the dunes Wull's feet sank and slipped so he went whaur the tide had been and the sand was firm. It was a lang stretch o beach. He watched the folk in the boats for a while till somebody cried 'Marion!' Jolted, he stretched his neck, but that Marion was a wee lass that had got her shoes weet.

Whaur the Lunan Water slunk across the beach he rolled up his troosers.

'Better gaein roond by the road,' somebody said. 'It's deeper than it looks.'

He squinted, for the sun was at its peak. 'Aye?' he said, 'Fairly that', and hung his boots roond his neck. As he scouted for a wey the current took the sand frae under his feet, carved a new, sharp bank, and he was in. The riverbed was covered in stanes: 'Jesus Christ Almichty!' Feet arched, he stumbled across, and – Jesus – that micht just be her back but he didnae want her tae see him like that, troosers up at his knees.

The lassie turned and the face was younger and though the hair was short there was nae fringe and it didnae matter wha it was saw him lookin like the eejit he was.

He sat for a while against the dunes. A fag aye helped him think, though the smoke chafed at his lungs.

Cissy had never brocht it up again, whitever it was. Well, so be it, he wouldnae beg. Maybe best he didnae ken. He flicked his tongue. The rings hovered, faded.

He wondered if she'd hae her cigarette holder, that had been his only taste o her, in Kelly Den, that day the burn had been swollen wi the rain and the licht had filtered through the young beech leaves? He'd sucked at the stem and played the donkey and she'd laughed frae her belly and he marvelled she had that in her, a wifie that had been the secretary o the Women's Guild, that read stories tae auld folk that were bedridden, that was makin a silk cushion for the kirk bazaar, and – he guessed – ate her denner frae china plates, and slept atween fine linen sheets.

It had just been him and her and it was as fine as the first time.

She'd laughed till she'd tae wipe the tears frae her een. 'Wull Greig,' – he'd taen the cigarette holder frae his mooth – 'You make me... do you ken, Wull, I havenae laughed for a long time.' The douceness aboot her face made him near forget tae breathe and maybe he could hae said somethin then but a look passed ahent her een. He held his wheesht, just handed the holder back and pointed at the wee flower enamelled on the trumpet end. 'Forget-me-not?'

'Edelweiss,' she'd said. 'I bought it in Geneva.'

Christ, he was daft, richt enough. If he didnae watch whit he was daein he'd hae nae fags left, and bugger all else he'd brocht for a picnic.

Against the drag o the tide the waves swelled, wavered and sank. The restless sea: nae solid under yer feet, nae sure and steady like the land – aye far ower much tae say for itsel. Anither and anither and anither wave, the backwash, like blood in his ears: that sound could dull a man's wits.

The dunes petered oot and the rocks began, and fewer folk had bothered their backsides tae walk as far, and that was a relief. He micht hae kent that was whaur he'd find her. Though he couldnae see her face, it was her. Nae anither lass on the beach like her. And even if he hadnae recognised the sheen on her hair, that neck, the shoulders, the length o the back, his hert-beat would hae tellt him it was her.

Just the twa men. But aye – bastard! – that was him, the ane she'd been oot walkin wi. Twa, three, ither women – the wife frae the tea shoppie, he'd expected that.

She was hardly scourin the beach for him, and it didnae look like there was much room on the rug. Her and her pal had their heids close thegither. Wull sat doon, his back half-turned, and watched the business o the schooner settin sail.

She'd maybe forgotten. She maybe hadnae meant it, the invitation – she hadnae thocht he'd come. The sound o her laugh made him turn his heid, but it wasnae him she was laughin at. She hadnae seen him, it was just… whit else would he expect, if she was enjoyin hersel, that she'd laugh?

The man Wull hadnae seen afore got tae his feet and studied his pocket-watch. Ae lassie stood up atween him and Miss Marion and sorted the pin in her bonnet. There was chit-chat back and fore, and though Wull couldnae mak oot the conversation, he heard 'station', and a whoop and there was anither lass on her feet, like she was in a hurry. The man made a show o brushin sand aff her claes.

Wull punched a fist intae the sand. 'God in heaven, dinnae tell me I'm ower late.'

The three on their feet linked airms. A chorus back and forrit, and they left. The man, in the middle, strutted his luck on his wee legs. They were that taen up wi ane anither they didnae gie Wull a glance as they passed him by. The twa women baith had the look o her, though the younger had the finer banes.

She was on her knees now, clearin things intae a hamper, but there was nae hurry aboot her – nothin tae say she'd tae catch the next train.

Christ, she'd as much as asked him. And if he'd picked her up wrang, well… Christ Almighty, whit was there tae lose? He got on his feet, straightened his tie, brushed himsel doon.

'Miss Marion?' – the question asked afore he was near enough, but she turned.

'Wull!'

He didnae need the wee squeeze o her hand tae ken she was glad.

Yon man was a mountain, and on his feet – nae ready, Wull thocht, tae welcome strangers at his picnic. But Wull kept his heid up and his een steady and held oot his hand, never let on he'd seen the twa o them thegither. 'Guid day, sir. William Greig.' But by God, if it came tae it, he'd put his fists up for her. Just gie him the chance!

'Robert Cunningham.' The baith o their grips as firm as the ither.

It cam tae Wull she was touchin his sleeve for his attention, strokin her thumb on his airm for his encouragement.

Her nails: he'd never seen nails like them, smooth and pink.

'It's a right bonnie day, Miss Marion.'

'Wull.' She took her hand awa. 'Please. I've told you before. It's Marion. Just Marion, to my friends.'

A wey in, that was all he needed, all he asked, please God.

'Robert, I told you about Wull. He's the one who saved me when, you know, that day… on the hills.'

'Pleased to meet you, Mr Greig.'

'Pleased tae meet you, sir.'

Marion took Wull's airm and turned tae her pal. 'And now, Margaret...'

A smile played aboot the lassie's lips. Anither ane that didnae want him there, but she hid it better. Her words rattled like frae the barrel o a gun.

'How d'you do, Mr Wull Greig. I'm Margaret. Marion's friend. Her very, very best friend. Well, I think I am anyway.' She dared Marion tae say different. 'We've known one another for a long time. Oh, goodness me' – an exaggerated expression for his benefit – 'I dread to think how long. The years fly! Don't you think so, Mr Greig?'

She minded tae shak his hand. 'I'm so delighted to meet you. I've heard so much about you – how brave you were, putting yourself at such risk... so resourceful.'

O'er-mindful o her thanks, and he got the feelin it wasnae for him tae hear.

'Marion was so lucky. I still can't believe how lucky. That you were there, I mean. It was such a co-incidence. We were all so glad you were there.'

Her gash-gabbit and him that couldnae put twa sentences thegither: if ane was worse than the ither, wha was tae say? There wasnae a soul on this earth was perfect or they wouldnae be here on the earth. There was maybe things aboot him Miss Marion wouldnae like tae hear aboot, and lassies – ach but he'd been a young man then and that was whit young men did. But if she... if he... if a man just got one chance, by God, this was it.

'Enough, Margaret!'

'Oh! Just listen to her. Marion can be the most exasperating person – did you know that, Mr Greig? She's stubborn and…'

Marion leaned forward, hardly at all. Ye could find nae fault wi her expression but Margaret took heed o it and her voice lost something. 'What was I saying? Yes, she can be exasperating.'

'I'd say Wull knows that more than anyone, Margaret.' Nae edge tae her; casual the wey she took ower; and just that wee gesture when she catched his gaze: 'It's grand tae see you, Wull. I'm so pleased you came.'

'I'd tae bide in Arbroath langer than I expected.'

But Margaret wasnae ready tae step back yet: 'You're Cissy Greig's brother, aren't you?'

She kent fine, it was clear, but he gied her a nod.

'And… is Cissy well?'

'She is.'

Margaret had heard Cissy was movin tae Dundee.

'I wouldnae ken that. She daesnae confide much in me.'

'Well, anyway, I do hope you're going to join us, Mr Greig?' Margaret gestured tae the travel rug. 'Robert, will you help me?'

It wasnae Wull's choice tae sit, but he was shy yet o offerin tae tak Marion for a wee walk.

Robert shook the sand aff the rug then spread it back on the sand. 'Mr Greig will have come to Lunan with his own friends.'

'I… I left them fishin.' Wull pointed across the bay.

Marion gied him a look.

'What I mean is, I was wi them. Left them at Ethiehaven, though – tae mak their ain wey. I tellt them… told them I wanted tae walk the length o the beach. I've never been at Lunan afore. Nae afore the day.'

'Robert...' Marion gied Robert a gentle push. He stepped aside.

Wrapped roond her wee pinkie.

'And Lunan Links is such a bonnie, bonnie place tae be, Wull. Why do you no sit for a while and enjoy it?' She set hersel doon and pulled in her skirts, stroked the rug aside her. 'Here, look. There's plenty room.'

Even a man wi little hope would think she was flirtin. Near as dammit, by God and – Margaret went tae help Robert strap up the hamper – didnae even care wha saw it: wanted them tae see.

He hadnae been as close tae her since they were up on the hill and that was surely the same ghost o a scent. 'I'd a friend, once, a young lady, spoke very highly o Lunan Bay,' he offered.

Margaret barged back: 'Such a shame you didn't get here earlier, Mr Greig,' she said. 'We'd a lovely picnic. Marion's sister Ethel made ham and mustard sandwiches with lots of butter.'

'Aye?' He couldnae summon enthusiasm.

'You've just missed her. Amy too. Both her sisters... you knew Marion had sisters?'

A nod, again, all that was needed.

'And Walter – he's the new minister at the parish kirk – perhaps you saw them?'

'Well, I...'

'Can't you just see Ethel as a minister's wife, Marion? And Walter's so dependable. So attentive... and not without charm!'

'Perhaps too charming?'

'Well, a good match, I'd say. For all concerned.' Margaret let sand trickle through her fingers. 'It'll take the pressure of you.'

Robert was peerin at somethin through a magnifyin glass.

'Are you bidin at Cissy's, Wull?' She'd the knack o shuttin oot the ithers, makin him feel there was just the twa o them.

'Aye.'

'She'll be pleased.'

'You ken Cissy.'

'Agate,' Robert said and handed twa halves o a stane tae Marion.

'That's lovely Robert. How did you know what was inside?' She passed it on tae Wull. The pattern o lines minded him o lookin doon ower the land.

'Yes, a perfect couple. As for Amy – tagging along like a chaperone...' Margaret didnae like tae be sidelined. 'I can't understand it. In this day and age, for Heaven's sake.'

'Here, Margaret,' Robert said, 'Have a cigarette.' He passed roond a wee tin: Balkan Sobranie in fancy letters. Metal on metal scraiked. A man o few words: Wull liked that.

There was somethin like companionship in the wey the fower o them drew on the smoke. That gied Wull the courage, though his voice didnae come oot lichtsome like he tried for. 'And which ane o you is the chaperone here?'

Margaret picked loose tobacco frae her tongue. 'We don't need chaperones, Mr Greig.'

Heat crept up the back o Wull's neck.

'We make our own way in the world.'

Another excuse for Marion tae put her hand on his arm. 'We've been friends for so long, Wull, the three of us – well, we've known one another since we were in school. Our families are friends… our parents… oh, but they've all quite given up on us now, I believe.'

Robert said he was gaein for a walk by the cliffs.

'Wait for me.' Margaret scrambled tae her feet. 'I'll come with you, Robert.'

~

Marion couldnae bear the thocht o the train back: that crowded it'd been in the mornin, all thae folk squeezed in thegither. And it'd been sic a bonnie day, and for all the distance – the breeze in her back – and if she walked it'd clear her heid – no, nothin tae worry aboot, just the effect o the sun. If Robert and Margaret didnae mind? Wull would see her all richt. 'Won't you, Wull?'

He could hae been wrang, but he thocht Marion winked at Margaret. And it could hae just been a fluke that Robert turned his back. But he would hae found somethin tae say, if she'd just gien him the time.

As it was, she took his shrug as 'Aye'.

'But we'll walk tae the station wi Robert and Margaret?'

'Aye.'

'We need to leave now.' Margaret was gaitherin up her things.

'Just as well we've you to keep us right.' Marion managed tae get hersel atween him and Robert, took an airm o the baith o them. 'Wull, with Walter gone, you'll help Robert wi the hamper?' She looked frae the ane tae the ither. 'You'll find you've lots in common.'

Wull took ae handle, Robert the ither. The sand was loose and they'd mair need tae watch their feet than speak. Near the dunes they stopped for a rest. Robert struck a match, cupped the flame till Wull got a licht. Robert waved his fag at a great tract o purple bloom. 'Sea Lavender.'

'Aye?'

Robert said he liked the hills better than the sea.

'Aye?'

The twa women were well aheid, airm in airm. Marion hailed them – pointed tae a short-cut.

It was a narrow track, awkward wi the hamper. They walked ane in front o the ither, the hamper hittin Wull in the shins and bangin the back o Robert's knees. The twa o them cussed and Robert said – but wi nae bad feelin – 'Is that not just like her, to lead a man astray.'

'At least there's nae hill-fog.'

Robert wondered how could it be that every time he walked the Tolmounth the colours, the light, the feel o the place was different?

'Aye,' Wull said. 'Ye hae it there. Every time it's new.'

There was ither tracks the baith o them kent, through glens, ower moors and mountains. And though Wull would never hae believed it, Robert kent every gully and corrie, every flooer that grew in every nook and cranny.

'And ye'll be a fisherman?' Wull asked. 'A gentleman like yersel?'

Robert thocht the Southesk had the biggest trout and the worst gamekeeper in the country. That new man, a cocky bastard if ever there was! It wasnae that lang since Robert defied the runt and offered tae report him tae the Laird for his cheek. The memory that fresh his face near turned scarlet.

Wull said well maybe he wouldnae get awa wi the likes o that, he'd be up in front o a magistrate. 'I've my ain weys, though, tae earn a gentleman's respect.' He tellt Robert the very best pool for a salmon, and the very place tae stand.

'Hoy!' Margaret waved from the station.

'What does she want?'

'Just sayin they've arrived.'

'No, she wants something.' Robert had traivelled a bit and that was whit he wanted, tae see the world. There were places ye could trek and never see another civilised man – or woman – for weeks on end, just yer scouts and bearers. There were plants there – grasses and bushes and trees, the likes o whit he'd never seen afore. That was whit he wanted, tae see new things, aye something new. Couldnae be daein wi the same thing day aifter day. Thae countries in the far-east: he liked it there, in the wilds.

'Ye lose yersel,' Wull said, 'in the wilds.'

'And find yourself.'

'Aye, well, and maybe it's the same thing.'

They heard the noise o the train and saw its smoke, but kept a steady pace, and there was time enough for a shak o the hand when they'd got the hamper loaded. The guard touched his cap as he passed alang the platform, bangin carriage doors. Folk hung oot the windows for a last look at the bay.

Marion waved until the engine picked up speed. The train slipped roond a bend and disappeared. 'Like a snake,' she said, 'in the heather.' She linked in and said she didnae want tae walk hame yet, could they gae back tae the beach?

'That Robert's a fine man.'

'What Robert doesnae know about plants isnae worth knowin.'

'Doesnae bum aboot it though.'

'No.' Everybody was gaein in the opposite direction: hardly a soul left on the beach. 'We could be the last folk on earth.'

'We could, lass. Marion…'

'Aye?'

'What did ye tell yer pals?'

'About?'

'Me.'

'You saved my life. You're responsible for me now, remember?' He wished she wouldnae tease, but there was nae malice in it, he didnae think.

They came upon a wee stream tryin for the sea. Wi the low sun, ye'd hae thocht the tangled threids o seaweed alive.

The tide weel oot: wave patterns on the sand rippled like the water itsel. She pointed oot the arrow prints o a seagull, scattered pebbles embedded on the beach, broken razor shells. Looking at her feet, she followed a sand ridge, took his hand in hers for balance, stepped alang anither ridge… and anither, and anither. The nane o them went very far until they petered oot.

'When the tide comes in again, they'll disappear,' she said. 'Every one o them will be gone. Everything'll be different, the morn. And the day, this nicht, this minute – now – this is the only time ever, ever ye'll see thae patterns in this licht. See, it's changin, as I speak. Is there no something sad about that?'

He couldnae think aboot that, all he could think was that if somebody was tae see them, somebody up on the dunes there, right now, somebody watchin them, her haudin in like that, and the dusk startin tae fall, they'd think... thae thochts tangled in his heid.

Nearer the river were mair pebbles, scattered heaps o them: grey, pink, green. Scraps o driftwood, fragments o fishing nets, wisps o rope, blunted seagull feathers. The sun ahent her, her shape against the sky.

She turned his hand palm up and put somethin on it and looked him straicht in the face. 'Something for you,' she said, 'Wull Greig. A wee present tae remind you o this very – present – day'. Reckless in the wey she looked at him. The shard o china burned his palm but he couldnae tak his een aff her face.

'Marion.' He had a hunger tae crush her in his airms, smell her, taste her... but this was something ye couldnae rush.

She waited. The top layer o sand stirred, like the shimmer o a veil. The sea-grass dipped low and brushed at the earth. Its colour changed as it bent.

'The gloamin. It'll be dark afore we get back.'

'Fine you ken it never gets really dark this time o year.'

'Yer family'll worry.'

'I'm bidin at Margaret's the night.'

He turned ower the fragment o china in his hand, ower and ower and ower. The edges had been rubbed smooth by the sea.

'It's a willow pattern, Wull. Shall I tell ye the story?'

Gulls circlin in the bay spotted a shoal o fish. Them still on the sand stretched their wings. Marion and Wull watched the awkward run, the heavy lift, their speed and agility in the air as the birds soared and dived.

'Wull… that time we met in Kelly Den…' She knelt in the sand tae sift it through her fingers. 'Did ye follow me there?'

She was tryin tae mak it easy. He slipped the bittie china intae his pooch, wiped his hands on his breeks.

'Ye did, didn't ye?'

His hand in hers, she traced a line – grains o sand clingin tae it – richt tae his wrist.

'Nellie once read my hand. Tellt me I'd hae a long life, contentment at the end.'

'If she tellt ye that, ye'd better believe it. But is that all you'd wish for yersel? Contentment? Maybes ye could dae better?'

'What aboot Cissy?'

'Cissy?'

'I'd feel guilty, wishin for more. There's folk in greater need o wishes comin true than me.'

'Everybody has the richt tae wish.'

'I always used to wish I could sing like Cissy.'

'She could sing, richt enough.'

'But what I mean is, what do I need tae wish for now?'

'Whatever it is ye really want.'

'Oh, all right, I'll try. I wish, I wish…' She turned her back and it was easier like that, her shoulders in front o him. His hands found their wey tae rest on them.

'I wish folk would let me be… no, don't stop. I didn't mean you. You're different – you don't need me.'

He thanked the Lord she couldnae see his face.

'I wish I knew what to do wi my life. I wish I could go away, far away. I wish I was useful. Look at Margaret. She's in publishing. I could easily do somethin like that.'

'Like what?'

'Well, just somethin… somethin that'd leave a mark on the world. A teeny mark, it could be, a scratch, a trace, a shadow… that's not much to ask, is it? I could… at least, I suppose I could…'

The wey she turned, Wull's airm went across the front o her neck.

'The sunset, Wull! Look! If ye saw thae colours in a painting you'd think they couldnae be true.'

The horizon on fire: the sky in the west full o reds and oranges and greys and even a deep blue.

'I could write.' Her heid tilted back against his shoulder: 'Some women write. But it might not be enough, you know, to support myself, to be independent.'

He held his wheesht.

'I can write. I write well enough, people hae said that. I write poetry…' Her lips parted, the wey they did when she wasnae sure – he'd noticed it afore.

'Anyway, what would you wish for, Wull?' The baith o her hands catched at his airm and held it close.

'I'd wish…' He pushed the fingers o his free hand through her hair and the glints in it and the smell o sun and sea and her scent stronger here, close in ahent her ears, under her chin. He couldnae help himsel, let his body press against her. He couldnae wish for nae mair than this.

She didnae shove him awa. 'I'd a little brother once,' she was sayin. 'I wish he hadn't died.'

'Some things ye cannae change, lass.'

'Wull Greig, I'm tellin you all my secrets. See what you've started?'

'I like it, when ye speak.'

'I still wish I could sing – I could, before George died. I used tae sing, Wull… but maybe I told you that. Did I?'

'I could mak ye sing.' The tips o her nails gripped him.

'And I wish I could fly.'

'I could mak ye fly.'

'Don't ever love me, Wull Greig.'

CHAPTER 4

Dinnet, Aberdeenshire: October 1899

Folk aye glad tae be thegither wi pals and neighbours for a dance and a cuppie: a laugh wouldnae gae amiss either, especially on a nicht black as the ace o spades, cauld enough tae shame winter.

Wull rolled his sleeves above his elbows, picked his fiddle up. He let his fingers slip up and doon its neck, stroked the curve o its belly wi a thumb. The angle o the bridge was grand. A twiddle o the bow screw, then he tested the strings, tuned the E up, played a chord.

How the tone had mellowed ower the years! Every time Wull played he gied thanks tae the Lord that his pal Jock Gunn had turned oot tone deif and Jock's fiddle had come his wey. He'd still been in short breeks then: it was that lang ago.

The noise in the hall faded. For Wull, there was nothin in his heid but the music, that he was ready tae try on his fiddle.

'That's a richt waltz, Wull. Ane o yer ane?' Aleckie was rubbin his hands thegither for warmth.

'Just an inklin o a tune yet. I've heard the melody in my heid but...' a wry look. 'It's just how it hangs thegither, man... that defies me yet.'

'Ach, man, when its time comes, when it's ready...'

'Aye, and for now we'll better get ready for the good folk o Dinnet.'

He was willin her tae come – like he aye did – the same wey his mither had willed the fiddle for him. But he hardly had need tae: that was near enough six months, and she'd never let him doon, never. She liked tae hear him play – had tellt him as much – loved the wey he made folk dance tae his tune. Dammit, he wouldnae tak a thing for granted, but there was every chance he'd be the happiest man in the country afore the nicht was oot.

The door opened. He looked across but his een were dazzled by the gasolier and he couldnae mak oot wha was there. The wind had got up, though, ye could hear it in the beech. Leaves – crisp and curled and the colour o her hair – flurried intae the hall wi a press o women, happed in shawls against the cauld. They stamped their feet, got in wee huddles, then fled as far frae the door as they could. There were cries o welcome and open airms, wee courtesies and waves o guidwill, but nae Marion.

Aleckie tested his drumsticks.

The dancers took notice: a hush.

'Richt, lads?' Wull said. 'Gay Gordons? The usual? G?'

They nodded.

'4/4.'

Sic a buzz then, as partner sought partner and the dancers took up position, that he missed her steppin ower the threshold.

But there she was: eager, just – if ye kent whit ye were lookin for – there was the slightest wariness as her een swept the company tae check the faces.

Wi the fiddle under his chin, the band at his call, and her barely ten yairds awa, Wull played a chord that made the very air above his heid vibrate.

Aleckie battered at the chair seat and they were straicht intae 'The Star o Robbie Burns'. Wull's heel tapped the flair and his wrist went like buggery. His bow flew ower the strings and his fingers danced that quick his brain didnae even try tae keep up, though his lugs aye checked that the resin gripped. Every note he played was pure.

Bert wasnae that sure o the accordion yet, aye keepin his heid doon, watchin his fingers on the buttons. The twang o the Jew's harp in the back: Jimmy just a young lad, but by God he could mak it dirl.

Tune followed tune: the dance-floor a swirl o purple and green and grey and blue – the dominie in his Cameron kilt dancin wi her in her broon frock wi the diamond pattern. But for now it was Wull that kept the band thegither and – eyebrows raised, a backward jerk o his heid – '"Cock o the North" comin up, lads.' 6/8 – a change o tempo.

They kept the pressure up: reels, jigs, polkas. Some o the tunes took Wull back tae his years on the road: the moor o Rannoch, the great lonely peaks o the west, the Atlantic jaupin at the foot o cliffs. Some minded him o the pleasures he'd had wi his mither's folk: the smell o woodsmoke, the wey Nellie'd wave – 'Come in aboot the fire, laddie.'

A waltz, and it got aff affa well wi 'The Northern Lights' – the first real tune he'd ever mastered. She swirled roond the flair. Wull minded how he'd played it for Miss Violet all thae years ago, against the noise o horses' hooves and the rattle o harness. She'd lifted her petticoats and twirled in the cobbled yaird, careless o the mud and the horse dung and the smell o the midden.

Marion was game tae, gie her that, and as comely – and aye that inclination o the heid. Nae lack o willin partners. He fancied she smiled everytime the new postmaster – as fat and wee a man as ye were ever likely tae see – tried tae birl her under his airm.

The folk were hungry for his music and Wull was in a fever: his oxters, the inside o his elbows, the palms o his hands and the cleft o his backside were runnin wi sweat. He could hae wrung oot his collar, but in atween the dances there was nae time but for a dicht o the nose on the back o his hand, and a wipe o damp fingers on the side o his breeks.

At the end o the Lancers, a smell o tea and the clatter o cups: the band looked tae Wull. 'Twenty minutes, lads.' He plucked the broken hairs aff his bow and cast them aside.

A crush at the tea urn till the dominie's wife got them sorted: a queue for tea and sandwiches; the bairns clamourin for lemonade, she sent tae the kitchen. The young ploughmen flooded ootside, left the door open in their hurry. The cauld soughed in till somebody had the presence o mind tae slam it shut. The rumbles o discontent that threatened died a sudden deith.

She was conversin wi the postmaster – him again. The twa o them took their cups tae the far side o the hall.

A young lassie brocht Wull his tea, near enough the wey he liked it. He mingled on the flair, nodded and smiled and spoke tae a wifie that had come frae Aboyne just for the dance, when she kent it was his band. But all the time Wull kept an ee on Marion and whit she was daein. He landed up on the edge o a knot o folk, near enough he could hear her voice, and by God it fair sparkled against the postmaster's drone. They drew ane anither aboot the poetry o Lord Byron, but she didnae agree wi him, and it was some comfort that she didnae bend tae his wey o thinkin.

His blood still thumpin through his veins: he tellt himsel tae calm doon and drained his cup. The bit paper was still there, in the pooch o his shirt, he could feel it. Folk near him moved on and left him standin by himsel, an empty cup in his hand. She was comin ower. He stroked his chin whaur he'd hacked it wi the razor.

'Wull Greig. How are you?' The hand offered tae him, pale against his, the lang fingers…

'Miss Marion!' He barely kent how tae dae this cairry on, like it was a game, but 'needs must' she'd said. 'How fine tae see ye.'

She fingered her pearls. They sat in a square neckline, edged wi tucks. Glass buttons frae neck tae waist. 'Wull Greig.' She said it again, her hand on his airm, just friendly like, folk would think, but he could feel the pressure o her thumb.

He wondered at how she could keep it up. Him – he aye felt like he'd explode.

'Congratulations to the band. It's an excellent dance. Everyone's enjoying themselves.'

Awkward, wi the cup still in his hand: 'Thank ye kindly.
Aye, they're a good crowd. But, yoursel now… you'll hae come
through frae yer cousin's place in Aberdeen? Been walkin the
hills?'

'I do so love the Hill o Fare. It's a special place for me. But bit-
terly cauld the day.'

Her een blue as the sea at Lunan Bay.

'I thought a dance would be just the thing.'

'I noticed… I see ye met the new postmaster.'

'An interesting man. Well-read. Keen to debate. I liked him.'

'But eh… aye, I've heard he's very…' It wouldnae dae tae bad-
mooth the man. 'And – ye're nae gaein back tae Aberdeen the
nicht, are ye?'

'I don't like that last train. It gets into the city far too late.'

'So…?'

'I'm lodgin at the inn.'

The floorboard at the top o the stairs creaked.

He was guided by the flickerin crack under the door, felt for
the handle wi ae hand as he gied ae wee rap wi the ither and
didnae wait for an answer – nae that anybody else would be up
here. The handle turned easy enough, though the hinge o the
door needed grease.

His heid near scraped the ceilin and he could just aboot touch
the fower walls if he stood in the middle o the room. A teenie
windae on the gable wall framed the black nicht. But there was

a box bed, a banked-up fire in the grate, and candles burnin bonnie. She was brushin her hair. He held oot his arms.

'Mind and lock the door, Wull'

'Christ, sorry lass. I'm nae thinkin straicht!'

'It's all right.' She shuffled up on the stool, so their twa faces were thegither in the mirror.

He set his arm across her shoulders and swayed in time tae the music in his heid.

'It's a shame I never get to dance wi you, Wull.'

'The fiddler's widow.'

'Is that whit they say? But look, our shadows are dancin.'

'Ye liked the dance though?'

'It's almost like flying, isn't it, when ye've a good partner?'

'The postmaster?'

She shrugged.

'Ye must be gey weary. Ye was never aff yer feet.'

'Keepin an eye on me, were you?'

'I'm richt glad ye came.'

'The landlord's gettin tae ken me well enough:' a smile that almost wasnae a smile.

A draught rattled at the window, made the candles flicker.

'I'll sort that.' Wull pulled the shutters to, dropped the hasp in place. The sound o the wind faded.

'That's better. Thank you. Did ye see the new moon, Wull?'

'Aye.'

'On its back?'

'Aye.'

'And the auld moon in its airms?'

'Aye.'

'Sign o a storm, is it nae?'

Wull kissed the side o her neck. 'Tis that, lass.' He loosened his collar and twa buttons o his shirt and tried tae pull her close.

She drew a line wi her finger whaur the mahogany o his neck met his white chest.

'Ye'd surely like tae slit my throat?'

'Wull!'

'Is there somethin up, though?'

She rubbed at the corner o an ee.

'Marion' – he drew oot the name oot. 'Marion, Marion. Are ye… I mean, I can… I'll nae bide, if ye dinnae want me tae?'

'No, no, Wull. It's nothin like that.' She lifted his hand tae her lips and held it there ower lang.

'But is there… there's somethin wrang, lass.'

'No, no. I came here o my ain free will. I want tae see you. And it was a good dance. I love tae hear ye play. It maks me feel alive.'

He reached for a candle and set it in front o them on the mantlepiece. 'Just, ye seem a wee bit…'

'I've been thinkin, Wull…'

His stomach turned tapsie-teerie.

A field o lang grass, and they mak a den in the midst, him and Miss Violet, the twa o them tired oot. Half asleep, the pair o them, her heid on Wull's airm, his een shut against the sun. She pokes him wi her finger and points at the sky. 'Look! Shapes in the clouds – a butterfly and an bird!' She asks Wull whit he sees.

An arrow and an anvil and an axe.

A lark rises. Somebody's in the field.

She touches Wull's lips wi a finger. They listen tae the lark soar.

'They've gone, Wull,' she cuddles intae him. 'Whoever it was.'

'Shush!' He puts his airm across tae haud her still.

'I've been thinkin, Wull...',

'Sh!'

She pulls him towards hersel. 'I love you, Wull Greig.'

Wull's faither stumbles across them.

He minded that nicht. It was the belt, thrashed him tae within an inch o his life, it felt like. For his ain guid, lest he get ideas.

'Wull?'

'Aye, lass?' That was the last time his faither ever lifted a hand tae him.

'I just want tae say, this – this bein wi you – it's been grand... what a summer I've had.'

'We've had.'

'Aye, you and me. Bonnie, bonnie days. And easy, wasn't it, in the good weather, tae meet on the hills? All thae places you took me, the long, long days, when we did nothin but tramp the heather.'

'And lie thegither.'

'We hardly saw another soul.' She took his hand in hers. 'But Wull, it's going to be harder in the winter, isn't it? This dance here and that village hall... this inn or that inn... and folk aren't stupid. They're bound tae talk after a while.'

He took up the poker tae riddle the fire and only when that was done tae his satisfaction did he face her. 'Let them.'

'Wull… you can guess whit I'm gettin at, can't ye?' The surge o heat frae the fire forced them baith tae lean back. 'I dinnae think we can keep on the wey we're daein.'

'Oh lass, ye're richt! I think the very same.' He gripped the taps o her airms. 'There's nae need for nae lies. I aye kent ye'd see the richt wey o daen. Fine ye see, wi thae een o yours' – his lips rested on each ane in turn – 'that nae guid ever comes o tellin lies.'

'I'm sorry, Wull.'

'The fault's mine, lass, bein quiet ower lang for fear ye'd turn me doon!' Haudin her at airm's length – 'there's nae future in it this wey, but it doesnae need tae be like this. We can hae a future.'

'My arms, Wull. You're hurtin.'

'This isnae just a fling for me, lass. I'm affa fond o ye.'

She studied the flames for a while. 'But Wull, it's no as simple as that.'

'What d'ye mean? How come?'

'We're no like that. The neither o us.'

'Like what?'

'You ken what I mean. Like other folk.'

He stood up but there was nae room for him tae pace. 'No, I dinnae ken. What d'ye mean?'

'We like our freedom. The baith o us.'

'We will be free, lass! That's just what I'm tellin ye! We can be free o the lot o them. Thegither, just me and you.' Finger pointin – 'you and me, me and you.'

'Do ye hae a cigarette, Wull?'

He put ane atween her lips. 'The neither o us is as young as we was.'

'No.'

'Oh, lassie, lassie.'

She offered him a draw. He took the fag and stubbed it oot. She let hersel be led tae the bed, climbed under the covers. Her heid sank in the feather pillow, her fingers fidgeted wi the sheet whaur it turned back on itsel. Not a word passed her lips.

He was all thumbs till his claes made a pile on the flair.

The springs o the bed jangled as he lay aside her. The baith o them rolled intae the middle. 'It's playin a polka for us, Wull.'

He held her face in his hands and wondered: he'd never seen her lie sae quiet. His hands took on a life o their ain: the shape o her chin, the line o her neck and her shoulders.

She said nothin mair till he rolled her on her side and stroked her back and then she said, in the voice he'd waited for, 'Oh, I like that, Wull.'

He moved closer and smoothed the flatness o her belly and followed the curves o her hips and her thighs and she was on her back again and his hands up atween her legs, and he cried 'Marion!' as he found her, though he didnae mean tae. The weight o him pressed her deeper intae the mattress.

A noise like a cough as she clung tae the cheeks o his arse and moved against him. Wull cried for mair, mair, mair but she hardly made a sound.

The twa o them stirred wi the noise o revellers bein thrown oot o the inn. Her smell was in him, on him, through him, ower him. She unravelled her legs.

'Ye all richt lass?'

'Mm.'

Still entwined: 'ye're better than this, lass. Ye deserve better.'

'I'm all right.'

'Ye was quiet.'

'We have tae be quiet, Wull.' She pushed him aside, turned her back. 'That's what…'

Wull slung his legs ower the edge o the bed. 'Ach, but I dinnae think it's that, ava, is it? It's just me. I dinnae hae the richt words for ye.'

'I dinnae need fancy words.'

'Just sometimes, or even if it was once in my life, I'd like tae be able tae say… somethin… somethin ye'd tak heed o.' He rummaged amongst his claes on the flair. 'But… listen, Marion… no, dinnae say nothin now. There's somethin I need tae say.' He took the bit paper frae the pooch o his shirt. The edges were stuck thegither wi sweat but he prised them apart and straightened oot the folds.

'I want somethin better for ye. For us. Look. Here. I want tae show ye this.'

She propped hersel on an elbow.

'It's frae last week's Courier.'

South African War
Volunteer Militia training at Cupar

'Nae that! The ither side.'

'What am I lookin for, Wull?'

'There.' He pointed tae an advertisement.

CANADA

Allan Line Shipping Company

Cheap fares from Liverpool

Monthly sailings

'Weel, what d'ye think?'

'About this?'

'I could mak plenty money in Canada, I ken that. I could start a new band. Get a job in the forests.'

'You want tae go tae Canada?'

'I want us tae gae. A new start. I've asked aroond. It'd work oot fine. It's a grand country if ye're sparkie.'

She was taen aback, even he could see that.

'I've enough money, dinnae worry aboot that – mair than enough – tae cover the fares and hae a bittie left ower.'

'Oh, Wull! I've taken so much from you already. You've been so good for me – tae me.'

'And will be.'

'But… Wull, dearest, dearest man, it would never work.'

'Ye think I couldnae keep ye? I'm nae skint, ye ken, just because… ye wouldnae need a thing. And every damn penny I hae, I'd gie ye.'

'I couldn't do it, Wull.'

'I'll show you what you mean to me! I'll show you!' He picked up his breeks and rummaged in the inside pocket. 'Here, tak this. The maist precious thing I hae – tak it… go on, tak it. Tak it.'

She turned it ower and ower in her hand.

'My lucky penny. You keep it. Now dinnae shak yer heid like that…' He backed away. 'Keep it. I want ye tae hae it.'

'I won't take it. It's yours. And what I'm saying is nothing to do with money, Wull. Nothin.'

'Whit is it then?'

Fingers through her hair tae push it back: 'It's just, well, look, really, what did you expect me to say? This is all so sudden. And I've been thinking, I mean, I wasn't expecting… I thought we both were of the same mind. I didn't think we'd even see one another – in the winter months, anyway.'

'No, no, but it doesnae hae tae be the morn! I dinnae mean now, lass. Ye'll hae time tae think it through, dae whit ye have tae dae. We'll wait till the spring. April, maybe. Or May. That's what I thocht.'

'I cannae go, Wull. I couldnae do that.'

'Naebody in Canada would ken my mither was a Tinker.'

'What are you saying?'

'I'm nae guid enough, am I?'

'Fine you ken it's nae that.'

'What is it then?'

She put the cuttin frae the paper doon on the quilt. 'Look, I'm sorry.'

'Is it Robert?'

'Robert? Robert? Oh my God, Wull! Robert and I are friends.'

'I've seen the baith o you thegither on Elliot Sands.'

'So?'

'Ae day I cam tae Arbroath – tae seek ye oot. The pair o ye was at the auld wreck.'

'And?'

The first time he'd seen her riled.

'Let me be clear. Robert's my friend. My decision is nothing to do with Robert.'

'Well, what's wrang then? What is it? Is there somebody else?'

'You want to know every detail of my life now?' She was different hersel, speakin the English again.

'I didnae mean it like that.'

Mair exasperated than angry: 'You wouldn't understand, Wull.'

'Ye could try me, for God's sake. Ye think I've nae wit?'

Nothin o comfort in the silence atween them: 'Did I ever say anything that led you to suppose…'

Wull put his hands in the air tae stop her, butted in afore he heard whit he didnae want tae hear. 'Christ, Marion! Look, it's just that I… I'm smitten, for God's sake. That smitten, I cannae even think o a life withoot ye. And I thocht ye'd jump at the chance tae get awa, the wey ye've talked…'

'Light me that cigarette again, Wull.'

'Look, I dinnae need tae ask mair o ye, if ye dinnae want it. Nae mair than I hae. That'll be enough. We'll gang oor ain weys and sometimes we'll catch up – in the summer months, eh? I'll tak ye places on the hills: plenty ither places I can tak ye! I'll be yer guide, ye can sit wi yer wee notebook and write yer poems, just like we did. Ye'd like that, aye? And I willnae bother ye on the dark nichts…' His shooders drooped.

She patted the bed aside her. He sat wi his back tae her. 'Wull, Wull. Would you really do that for me?'

'Aye, but maybe if there cam a day…'

'Wull, of course you're right. Of course, I'd like to get away. It's what I've always hoped for. But I can't promise anything. I can't just walk away. Not now, when mama's not well. She worries so much.'

'Ye've twa ither sisters.'

'Aye, and that's the problem.'

'Just, I thocht this micht be the only chance we get and if we dinnae tak it…'

'Wull, I really need time to think.'

'Whit does yer hert say, lass?'

She was quiet. He turned tae look. Nae when she fell on the cliff-side and near tore her airm frae its socket; nae when her feet had been that sair wi blisters she couldnae walk anither step… he'd never seen her greet. But there it was, a tear stuck i the corner o her ee. At last she answered: 'I'm nae sure I hae a hert, Wull.'

'Oh, lassie.' He wrapped the baith o his airms roond her, pushed his face intae the fineness o her hair, and squeezed her as ticht as he could, tae stop his ain tears, for would that dae onie damn bit o guid if he was tae greet?

It was her broke the silence. 'I once wondered about going to Africa, to get away. Do you think I could have been a missionary?'

'A missionary? In Africa?'

'We've a link – our kirk – with a mission in Natal. They write, telling us about their work, asking for help. I'm sure I could've be useful there.'

'Holy Christ, Marion. Thae Zulus are fearsome. Dinnae think o gaen tae Africa.'

'Why ever not?'

'God, the black men fecht ane anither, the white men fecht ane anither. They'll all end up fechtin ane anither. Africa's a hell o a place, I dinnae want ye tae gae there.'

'I didn't want you to love me.'

CHAPTER 5

Arbroath: 20th February, 1900

Whether it was the cauld, whether it was bidin wi Cissy, whether he'd been dreamin… he couldnae get back tae sleep. And if there were things he still had tae dae, it was ower late.

He should hae gone back tae Dun.

Even if it had just been tae say cheerio tae the wee kitchen maid – hardly mair than a bairn she was, but a bonnie lass and a guid hert. He'd been fond o her: that he'd gien her not a thocht in the last twelve month was neither here nor there.

If there had been the time, he micht hae… but whaur did a man draw the line? If Dun, then why no Ballater? The widow had never done him nae hairm, and a lot o good. She must hae wondered whaur he'd gone. And Betsy. If he'd things tae say it surely should hae been tae her.

If it had just been him and her – he'd aye thocht that – things micht hae turned oot. That's what he'd say. But it was surely water under the brig, for if he went tae see her, and her faither or her new man catched him, they'd hae his guts for garters.

It wasnae easy tae get dressed under the quilt, but the air was that raw it was the only place tae be. It would hae been better for Cissy tae tak board money aff him, that wey he could hae put coal on the fire.

He'd hardly ever gien his fiddle box a second glance ower the years, just as lang as it did the job, but this was a different kettle o fish. The damp and the cauld and waves as big as hooses would be bad enough for the twa o them, never mind the fiddle. He took in the state o the wood, weathered since the day his faither made the box – fair's fair, a fine job he'd made. There was scratches on the varnish, a wee crack on the lid, the pins o the hinges loose: nothin he couldnae fix. The linin his mither put in – scraps o silk frae the big hoose, maybe even a frock Miss Violet wore, though the truth was he didnae recognise it. The material was ripped and faded, but the stuffin still followed the fiddle's curves and held it safe. Aye, the box was as guid as it needed tae be.

He took up his fiddle, set it under his chin. Habit a strange thing, he thocht, and plucked the A string. The note true and how would it nae be? Had he nae been constant tae his fiddle for mair than twenty year? Loyalty – love – that was whit a fiddle needed. He plucked again, louder than he meant, damped it doon wi his hand quick. He heard a B flat chord, and afore he kent whit he was daein, his fingers were findin the notes o his melody, though the bow was still in the box and his richt hand was keepin time on his thigh.

He laid the fiddle awa, took it in his heid tae check the date o the sailin. A peek in the envelope – Holy Christ, three days time, as if he didnae ken it already. And in twa months… April… they'd be there, God willin. Wha was tae say whit micht happen then?

Still nae sound frae ben the hoose.

He blew on his cupped hands. If Cissy had just banked up the fire afore she went tae her bed… but cauld or no, the letter, that was the next thing.

He found paper and a pen ahent the wee trinket on the mantlepiece, but his hand shook and his sighs were heavy as he tried oot 'my dearest' or 'my dear'. The first bittie paper got scrunched up and thrown in the bucket when it was near done because he wrote 'Yours sincerely', and didnae like it. He crossed it oot wi black lines and tried 'your affectionate'. That sounded richt but she micht think it presumptious, so he wrote 'kindest regards' and then 'very truly yours'. The neither o them looked richt on the page.

At last he made up his mind. Thank God Cissy had anither bit paper. He vowed no tae mak an arse o it this time.

The hale thing written oot again, he signed it 'Wull'. But she maybe didnae like him tae be ower familiar, or maybe he wanted tae be mair o a man o the world, sae he added 'Greig'.

Dear Marion

I must tell you. I have been informed by telegram that there has been a cancellation and we can have two berths on the 'Castillion', another steamer of

*Allan Line. It also sails from Liverpool. The date of
the voyage is 23rd (this month). That is not tomorrow
but the next day, in the evening. From what you said
last week I know you are ready (and impatient too),
so I took the decision and telegrammed back to say
we will go. I know it is much earlier than we planned
but it is a better ship than the April one and a better
berth. Anyway, I heard that the winds might be as bad
in April. It is often blustery then. And if we go now it
will give us more time to settle in Canada before the
winter.*

*Just bring one bag. You can send for your books and
things later.*

*The only problem is, I think it will snow, so we should
get to Glasgow as soon as we can. I have papers to pick
up there, then we'll go together to Liverpool.*

*I am biding at Cissy's house and have had to tell her.
She is none too pleased, but it is none of her business
after all. I'll wait for you here. Please come as soon as
you can.*

I am,
Yours aye
Wull Grieg.

He was vexed the last twa lines sloped up at the end... ach, but
that was nothin. The letter was guid enough, if a bit clippit. It
minded him o the wey the minister at Dun used tae speak – him

that was the height o a cuddy's arse and had tae stand on a box tae see ower the pulpit. Miss Violet and him, they'd laughed, when they were bairns, at the wey the hem o his cassock stuck oot like a lassie's frock.

He wondered if he should hae written he loved her – it was a word ye could write easier than say – but couldnae see whaur it would fit.

The travel papers... should he put hers in wi the letter? He thocht the better o it, and sealed the envelope.

Miss Marion Angus

In his best writin... he touched the name tae his lips and left it there for a lang time. There was naebody tae catch him at it.

The wag-at-the-wa chimed seven, a tinny chime.

Cissy coughed and spluttered ben the hoose, her lungs full o dust. Poor sowel that she was, gey thrawn that the life she'd hoped for had passed her by. And wha could blame her for that? But it was naebody's fault – nae unless their faither's, leavin the land for a job in the mills o Arbroath, hopin for ower much. It was just the wey the dice fell.

Maybe if Cissy could get awa and start again, he thocht. Maybe it'd be better for her in Dundee, if she got a job there, like she was hopin. Things'd pick up then. Somethin guid would come chappin at her door, somethin that'd turn her aroond. That's whit she needed.

He wouldnae like her nosin in his business though. Whit was

he tae dae wi his papers while he was oot? The fiddle box: he lifted the fiddle, slipped them in a split in the linin.

Ootside, it wasnae even the dawnin. He catched a whiff o asphalt whaur the road had been mended. Not a sowel tae see, just the echo o streets and him mair used tae the ring o an open road. At the kirkyaird, the gate was still locked. He louped the wa and his feet crushed a clump o snowdrops.

Just their twa names on the stane, and their dates, and that wouldnae tell ye nothin if ye hadnae kent them for yersel. Nothin o the days and the months and the years his mither cleaned and mended and wiped bairns' arses and noses and darned socks and patched troosers and boiled up her broth... nothin o the smell o it, the taste o her rabbit stew. Nothin o stories, and sangs, and laughs when they were all roond the fire on a Saturday nicht, nothin o the wey she'd smoothed Wull's broo that time he had the fever... nothin o... nothin o his faither's...

A taste o bile in Wull's moo.

'Blood will out.' His faither sneered, and the twa o them glowered at ane anither. His mither riddled the fire wi the poker till she near put the damned thing oot then stood up and said 'Well then, laddie. Naethin that happens that isnae meant tae be. There's worse things a man can dae than tak tae the road.'

She sorted his collar and brushed stoor aff his jaiket, careful nae tae touch the black bruises she'd soothed wi vinegar in the nicht. A pressure on his airms tae haud them doon and a wee shak o the heid, as she stood atween him and his faither.

'Just mind, Wull lad, haud yer heid up high and keep yer ee on the road aheid. And never wish ill on any man, or it'll come back tae haunt ye.' She pushed somethin intae his hand. 'Keep this and ye'll never want.' She put her lucky penny in his hand and steered him oot the door.

Moss was creepin ower the stane, but there wouldnae hae been a stane at all, if Cissy hadnae scraped the siller thegither for it somewey or ither. She'd worn hersel oot afore her time, she had, aye scrimpin and savin, and nothin tae show for it that he could see, but a tombstane.

Surely Cissy didnae blame him for every damn bit o bad luck they had aifter they left Dun: that hassle wi the hoose, the twa wee laddies getting the fever – poor wee sowels – his faither's blacklistin in the mills, his mither trampled by a run-awa heifer in Market Street? There was nothin he could hae done, even if he'd been at hame. And if his mither had passed on her luck wi the penny... he couldnae hae refused it, could he?

Och, but it'd work for the pair o them in Canada as it had worked for him. It meant somethin tae him, that Marion had kept it. He pulled his bonnet ower his ears and louped back ower the dyke, and that was surely the last time in his life he'd ever leave the pair o them.

The grip o winter was ticht: the abbey ruins staggered under the weight o clouds. In the High Street, the shops were shut and shuttered. Even the smell o the Brothock Burn – like a shit bucket – was frozen.

Canada – it was cauld enough there, in winter, tae freeze a

man's balls aff. But they said everythin was bigger: peaks ye couldnae scale, forests ye never found an end tae, lochs as big as the German Ocean. And great empty spaces o virgin soil for a man that was ready tae throw his roots doon.

The bells o the Fisherman's Chapel dirled their turn. Wull's tackety boots clipped a rhythm but the tune in his heid had mair o a flow tae it, like a waltz, the Pride o Erin.

Doh te doh soh fah ray me soh

He was minded o angels in heaven.

Dammit, Dun Kirk! Was that whaur he'd heard it afore? A line sung by the precentor for some psalm? Miss Violet peerin at him frae under her bonnet and him… in paradise.

At the crossroads wi Commercial Street, he looked this wey and that and went for the sea that was the colour o his mither's pewter teapot. Waves threw themsels at the harbour wall and swept across the fingers o rock that stretched frae the land. Decks on the boats were cleared: fish boxes lashed or braced, hatches battened doon, cables and lines fast.

The ruins o that damned hoose, like a warnin, at Danger Point.

Hardly a soul on Keptie Road. He'd surely catch her there, gaein tae the kirk, he was early enough. He'd raise his cap and she'd stop and speak, her voice would be steady and proper and polite – a marvel how she could dae that. He was gruff but he could be polite and her sisters would never see he was weak at the knees. They'd walk on likely, oot o politeness, and he'd tell

her himsel, then that it was done. That was the wey he'd like it
tae happen, for he'd see her face – the hope and the joy, now
she'd made up her mind.

But if the twa sisters didnae walk on he'd pass her the note
but whether he'd say 'I hae a note for you, Miss Angus' or 'I've
written a note for you, Miss Angus,' and hand it ower bold as
brass, or whether he'd slip it intae her hand when naebody was
lookin... he wouldnae mak up his mind till the moment.

He recognised her faither stridin doon, a fine figure o a man,
ye could see his breedin in the straicht back and the easy flow o
his stride, his character in the set o his face, aye even in the wey
he'd twisted his mutton chops. Wull lifted his cap and said 'Guid
morning, sir' and the man hailed him, squintin like he couldnae
quite mind Wull, but still, would hae stopped for a blether if he
hadnae been hurryin for the early mornin service.

Wull wished he'd gone man tae man, stood up for himsel.
Maybe her mither would hae had a fit, but yon was a reasonable
man. Riled at himsel for giein in, but it wasnae for lack o backbone, it was whit she wanted and he'd hae tae live wi that. When
they were settled and sent word back and her faither realised
Wull's intentions, well then... it'd be different then.

A brattle o thunder. The clouds were piled up, layer upon
layer, ower the sea. They pushed ane anither aside like currents
o a river. Flakes o snaw the size o feathers filled the air and
swirled like they never wanted tae settle. Wull could hardly see
twa inches in front o his nose and when he turned, couldnae
see whaur he'd been.

Her bedroom at the back o the hoose, her bureau at the

windae and usually that was whaur she'd be. It wasnae the first time Wull had stood under the big beech and waited for a sign. A patch o ground still clear o snaw on the lea side, the trunk wide enough for his back and skeleton branches low enough he didnae stick oot like a sair thumb. He heard the back door open, but couldnae see ower the wall: a bit o business wi a shovel. The door banged shut. It wouldnae be her, but it cheered him, that somebody was in.

Nae like Dun, but a fine hoose just the same. He'd get her a hoose like that some day. That was the kind o thing meant somethin tae a woman.

The steeple clock chimed the quarter past the hour – muffled in the snaw. He shivered some mair. Then the half past. Nae wey he could hae missed them. He'd hae heard the front door and their voices, and would hae seen them at the end o the road. They surely werenae gaein tae the service the day. He stamped his feet and thumped his airms, checked the windae. Not a swish o a curtain. The snaw near an inch deep already and that must be why the nane o them were oot.

He wondered what hairm there'd be in knockin at the door – there must be a chance she'd open it.

A bang frae the front o the hoose and that must be them and he was on the road afore the sound died awa, tae meet her at the corner. Her sister… nae jaiket, nae shawl, just a wee bolero and she was shiftin, shoulders jerkin like somebody was on her back, hardly lookin at him though he stepped richt in front o her.

'Excuse me, Miss.'

A muscle on her cheek twitched.

'Are you… ' Embarrassed tae catch her like this, lookin as if she'd been greetin, his smile was ower quick. Bein false didnae suit him, just put the baith o them mair on edge. 'Miss Angus?' She backed awa but kept her een on him, half shut lids, sizin him up.

'Why do you want to know?'

'It's just. Eh… '

'Where did you come from?'

'I was comin tae your house.'

'Who are you?'

'Wull Greig, Miss. Pleased tae meet you.' He touched his cap.

'What d'you want?'

He patted his pocket. 'I've a letter.'

'A letter! Why didn't you say so? Give it to me!' Her hand thrust at him.

Wull held back. 'I was wonderin if…'

'Give me my letter, please.'

'Sorry miss, I didn't mean…' His turn tae back awa. 'It's nae for you. It's for your sister.'

'My sister!'

'Miss, I'll better tak ye hame.' Wull's airm went oot tae steady her. 'Ye've just yer baffies on.'

She let him steer her alang the path, but came back tae her senses at the door. 'I'm all right now. Thank you very much. Give me the letter, and I'll see Amy gets it.'

'Oh, sorry miss, it's nae for Miss Amy.' He showed her the name. 'It's for Miss Marion Angus.'

'Marion! Dear God in Heaven, I thought you meant Amy.'

'Is Miss Marion in?'

'On a day like this? What would you expect?'

He held on and used the tilt o his heid tae suggest she micht get Marion. 'Could you? Would you mind? '

She folded her airms. 'My sister's indisposed. Do you want me to give her the letter or not?'

Still haudin the envelope in twa hands: 'Ye'll see she gets it though?'

Though he wore a groove in the flair atween the fireside and the windae, there was nothin but white oot there. He took the shovel frae the side o the fire and cleared the doorstep. The debris in the street, bits o tarpaulin happed ower roofs, heaps o coal and dust – years o heavy toil and sweat frae Robbie Dean's coal yaird, were all smothered in a white goon. Even the cairt wi the broken axle looked the better for a coverin, and for once there was nae sailors brawlin at the White Ship Inn.

Back tae the fire and he shifted the claes horse and set the front legs o his stool hard against the fender. Him and Marion… his fingers tapped on the stool, but he couldnae even think o the tune, just a ta, tatty, ta tatty ta tatty ta. Ower and ower, till Cissy said 'For the love o God, Wull.'

He stood up and his een catched the wee china trinket on the mantelpiece, the lassie's face tilted up at the minstrel like her hert would burst. It was the ane his faither had found in twa bits in the midden o the big house. Ye could hardly see the wee crack atween the shepherdess and the minstrel, whaur his faither had mended it wi white lead. His mither had been that proud o it at the time. 'That's you Wull, you and yer lass.' He'd blushed and looked awa, feared for whit his mither micht ken.

Cissy went tae trim the tilly lamp. A hiss, a circle o licht on the table, a smell o paraffin. 'Nearly oot, and that's the last.'

He went tae the windae. Snaw was piled half-wey up the pane. He'd gae up the road the morn, try again… he had tae catch her the morn. No, he'd said he'd wait, he'd better wait, trust she'd come.

Christ, the lassie would hae gien her the note, surely? Even if there was somethin on her mind – onie fool could see the state she was in – she'd hae gien Marion the note.

The air was still thick wi snaw and what if it didnae stop in the nicht? How had he nae thocht o that? He'd hae tae… tyach, he should hae thocht o that. Christ, if he was…and what if… his mind wouldnae settle. She needed a hand. She'd leave afore he got tae her hoose. He'd miss her if she went roond by Margaret's… she'd hae tellt Margaret, sure as hell. Would she? Robert? Would she hae tellt him?

He went tae poke the fire but Cissy stirred in her seat and he stopped himsel in time and just felt the weight o the poker in his hand. 'Ye want some coal on the fire, lass?'

'That'll dae a while yet.'

He rested an elbow on his knee, his chin on his hand.

'Ye were that sure she'd come.'

His foot tapped the seconds on the flair.

'It's a big thing ye're askin.'

'Christ-sake, Cissy, she'll come.' The legs o his stool scraped the flair. He went back tae the windae and lifted the curtain: the black mongrel bitch frae next door the only thing in the road. 'She has a mind o her ain.'

'Dinnae worry yersel, I ken that.' Cissy's face as torn as the sheet she was mendin: 'but that's nine o'clock.'

'The last train awa.'

'Oh, aye! Expert on the timetable, are ye?'

Wull unlaced his boots. Nothin else tae be done the nicht. He should hae kent she'd need time. He hadnae… he shouldnae… the neither o them had thocht it'd be that quick. But three days in hand, he tellt himself. There wasnae much o it, but there was time if he catched her in the mornin.

A bang at the door: Cissy gied him a look and picked up her things. Wull pushed his hand through his hair. 'Holy Shit! I never meant her tae bide the nicht, Cissy.'

'Stir up onie kind o shit, and ye never ken whit'll happen.' Cissy went ben the hoose and slammed the door.

Well, thank the Lord. She'd come, and he'd think o somethin, he would, he'd think o somethin.

The door opened: snaw drapped at his feet. The bitch had shat on the doorstep, and it was Rev. Angus stepped across it and passed Wull by wi nae mair than a nod o the heid till he shook the snaw aff his coat and his boots. Just ae set o footprints tae the door and not anither soul in the street, and whit could Wull dae but follow him?

He said he wouldnae sit, thank you very much and he hoped

Wull's sister was well for she'd let her membership lapse, and that was a great pity, but the kirk aye welcomed folk back tae the fold. Now. He'd come straicht frae the evenin service. There was business tae be dealt wi and he hoped this wasnae a bad time? Wull braced himself against the mantelpiece but the man's voice was douce and he didnae look in a state. Maybe it'd be for the best.

'I might as well be blunt. There's no easy way.' The voice still measured. 'Mr Greig, you'll be a reasonable man. And a man of the world. I can talk straight. My daughter was most distressed.'

'Aye?' But he'd seen that for himsel.

'She's gone away.'

He'd just asked her tae gie ower a letter. 'I dinnae ken whit ye're speakin aboot, sir.'

'She doesn't want you to know where she's gone.'

'You mean... I think you're makin a mistak.'

'It's no mistake. Marion doesn't ever want to see you again, doesn't want any contact, of any kind, with you.'

'Marion?'

'No prospect of... unless – until... complete and utter...' The maist o the words went ower Wull's heid, just every time the man said 'Marion' it put a catch in his chest, and at 'far away' he saw her, caught in no-man's land, spears flyin through the air above her heid, sodgers advancin wi firearms at the ready. He couldnae speak.

'Whatever impression you had of Marion, Mr Greig, her personal allowance is small.'

Whit was he meant tae say tae that?

'She has been accustomed to a good life – thanks to the generosity of an aunt – but that's going to change.'

The chill o cauld stane through his feet. Not a flame left on the fire, or a flicker o heat in his belly. Would the man never shut up? And Cissy ben the hoose, had she brocht this on him? She didnae want it tae work, did she? She'd warned him it didnae dae, mixin wi toffs.

Ae hand made a fist. He covered it wi the ither.

'Perhaps you mistook her gratitude...' The man's fingers twiddled a ring on his pinkie. 'Shall we agree, then, Mr Greig, a misunderstanding?'

Wull found his tongue. 'I need tae see her.'

'She doesn't want to see you.'

'I'd believe it if I heard her say that.'

The man drew himself up, hands thegither, like he was in the pulpit, just the points o his fingers touchin. 'Mr Greig, I didn't want to have to do this, but she's sent you a message.' He took Wull's envelope frae his pocket and turned it upside doon. His letter, torn tae shreds, scattered ontae the hearth. There was a glow here and there as the fragments touched the cinders.

The minister was still speakin. 'And if we agree that's an end to it, I'll make no official complaint.'

The set o Wull's face changed. He reached for Cissy's fags on the mantelpiece.

'I'll ask God's forgiveness, for you both, of course. The bringing of this – this affair – into the light of God's truth is the first step towards redemption, for you and for Marion.'

That catch again, in Wull's chest.

The minister's fingers moved apart, thegither. 'Sin is most to be dreaded when it's hidden, buried away, out of sight, in the recesses of a man's heart.'

Wull's hands shook. He tapped the matches on the packet o fags and put them doon again. 'I didnae think it was a sin tae love.'

'Ah, but "love"… what is that? What kind of love? Duty, responsibility… they are the greater love. You may not know, Mr Greig, but Marion's mother is in delicate health. And – in the very near future – we expect her sister to get engaged to a man of the cloth. Marion doesn't wish any scandal that'd cause unhappiness, or shame her family – or jeopardise her sister's happiness.'

'And her happiness?' There was nae wey for his anger tae gae but intae his fists.

'I think she's demonstrated, by her actions, where she sees her happiness. Mr Greig, perhaps… this is not the first time Marion… I'm here with her welfare in mind.'

The tilly lamp spat at the twa o them.

'If you care for her in the slightest… I'm quite prepared to – let's say – compensate you. In the circumstances…'

The licht sputtered oot in a reek o paraffin. Shadows leached intae ane anither. His mither's wee ornament, that was in Wull's hand ae second, shattered against the far wall the next.

Ootside, snaw covered every track.

CHAPTER 6

Arbroath: 31st March, 1900

Ethel doesn't look up when Amy comes in. Amy ignores Ethel, but, to my surprise, gives me a nod as she heads for the bookshelf. I button up my cardigan against the chill air she brought in.

It's the society pages of the weekly magazines she usually reads, yet, here she is, feigning interest in reference books. I slide my 'diary' under the blotter and pretend I'm working on the half finished – actually, barely started – poem underneath.

Blossom on the blackthorn bush
Bonnie blossom...
White blossom on the blackthorn

Like snow – snaw/sna?
White – for a bride (?)
                    morn, born,

forlorn, torn, worn

black thorns

tear at (scart)

vicious/malicious

A travesty, to use the word 'poem'. All I have is an image. The contrast of it shocked, yet appealed to me – something of the old ballads in it. If I could only do it credit… not yet, not now, there's too much happening. But I won't throw it away. I've no idea how – or if – I'll ever use it. But I will be a poet.

In their last congegational letter, the missionaries said that native people make images of goddesses to protect their villages, little statues of their enemies in order to control and destroy them. Isn't that something like what a poet does?

Patterns on sand (land, hand, band)

Disappear wi(th) the tide (wide, hide, chide, reside)

Cycles of nature/ cyclical/ ephemeral

things you can't change… Things ye cana (?)(cannae?) change…
Dies, (lies, relies…wise?)

Be careful what you wish for
Mind what you wish for

The future – entices
(crisis!)

Wish/dream? Hope? Pray? (same or different?)

This is ridiculous.

But I should add 'belief' and 'faith.' After he read that last letter from the missionaries, papa built his sermon around the power of faith – 'faith as small as a mustard seed' – St Mathew's Gospel? – enough to move a mountain.

'What's for ye, willnae gae by ye.' That's what Nellie would have said.

'Marion?'

I'm about to ask her opinion but judge she won't find the mystical, spiritual power of belief at all fascinating. 'Yes, Amy?'

Her smile barely crinkles the skin.

'I missed you while you were away.'

I pinch the top of my nose, hoping to convey my disbelief without being too rude. Holding the position for a count of ten should remind her I hate someone hovering nearby while I'm writing. 'I've only been away four weeks.'

'And Aunt Tweedie?' She plays with the button on her cuff.

Five more minutes of peace: that's all I need. I read the last few sentences I've written again. Just something to round it off. One last paragraph, dear God, that's all, but I need it now, if I'm to meet the deadline. I've never missed one yet, and don't want to with my last submission. A sentence, even, will do, as long as it's the right one.

Bringing my little newspaper column to a premature end has been more difficult than I expected. Not because it's my first ever real 'work', not even because, thanks to my 'nom-de-plume', I've had the pleasure – unaccustomed pleasure – of saying exactly what I want. It's not even the frisson of doing something mama and papa would disapprove of, nor the secret notoriety – though I will admit to fanning the speculation, putting forward decisive arguments to prove the author is a man. No, it's none of these things.

God help me, I know it's all a fiction, with the merest sketch of a plot. But my characters have developed personalities, quite taken on a life of their own. I like 'Christabel': admire her independence, charm, wit – her love of life, of literature. Even 'Arthur', I've a certain affection for, despite his inability 'to see himsel as ithers see him' – that's not quite what the bard said, but the sentiment's right. And so I've had more sleepless nights over abandoning these two, than I've had over leaving my own sisters.

It wasn't that I planned an 'Arthur and Christabel lived happily ever after', ending. Yet I'd like to… if I could bring things to a conclusion with… no, just a hint that the relationship might end well. Something unfinished, that'd be perfect.

'You weren't very keen to go': a pained expression in the eyes, Amy's attempt at sympathy.

I don't mean to sigh: my voice acquires an edge in attempting to set the record straight. 'I didn't mind at all. I always enjoy seeing Aunt Tweedie. It was just the urgency of it, and the rush for the train that took me aback.' I refrain from telling her the blessing it turned out to be, taking me out of the town, helping me to pass the last four whole weeks.

'I was glad papa didn't tell me to go.'

Much good she'd have done.

'Anyway, it'll be the last...' I leave the sentence hanging. My chin rests on my hand, which covers my mouth until I compose my thoughts. 'Someone of her age, I mean. You never know.'

'She was that bad?'

'No, I didn't mean... there was nothing much wrong, actually, by the time I got there.' I decide to try again, lay my pen along the spine of the notebook and give Amy my full attention. I can surely spare her a few minutes. I wouldn't like her to remember me unkindly. 'After the telegrams that went back and forth that day I thought she must be at death's door. But no, she seemed tired, a bit off-colour, that's all, just what you'd expect at her age. I don't understand why papa got into such a panic.'

Amy paces to the window and back, conscious all the while of the impression she's making.

'For Heaven's sake, Amy, you look as if you're about to burst. What is it?'

'Nothing!' Instead of fiddling with the button she pushes at the cuticle of a nail. 'I don't know what you mean.'

'Good heavens! How did that happen?'

I'd forgotten Ethel was in the room. She's inspecting her embroidery through a magnifying glass. Her pose reminds me of a picture in one of my very first books. 'Be good, my maid, and let who will, be clever', was the caption. I never liked the implication.

'Has one of you interfered with my work?' That's her first acknowledgement either of us are in the room.

I shrug.

Amy throws up her hands. 'Don't look at me! Not guilty!'

I decide to retreat: tidy my papers, slot my thesaurus back on the shelf. My hand wavers. I withdraw the book again, flick through it. Robert's signature on the frontispiece: 'on the occasion of...' he can be so damned formal at times. I decide to make room for it in my bag.

'Marion, you're not off somewhere again, are you?'

A moment's apprehension: but she's whining, not accusing. She knows nothing. 'Into town,' I say. 'Right after lunch.'

'You're more often out than in.' She leans towards me and drops her voice to a whisper. 'Actually, I did want to ask you something. In private.'

Not a sound do I make, but my lips exaggerate the shape of the words and my eyebrows ask the question. 'What about?'

'I know you think I'm foolish.'

'I'd no idea you'd such insight!'

'See? You're always making fun of me.'

I give a down-at-the-corners smile. 'Just teasing.'

'What you don't realise is how mature I am now. Well, why would you? You're not interested in me and you're never here.'

I retrieve my cigarettes.

'Mama doesn't like you smoking.'

'You want one?' I offer the packet.

'Of course I don't. You think I want horrid stained fingers? You're a disgrace, Marion.'

'That what you wanted to tell me?'

Ethel's voice: 'Heaven's sake, you two. Stop your bickering and let me concentrate. I'm having to take out every single stitch I've done this morning.'

'Ethel, if you need a magnifying glass to see the mistake, I'm sure no-one else is going to notice.'

'As if I'd take advice from you! Miss Marion Slapdash-get-it-done-as-quickly-as-I-can. Your stitch-work is a disgrace, for someone in your position.'

'My position?'

'You've had every advantage.'

'My stitch-work? It isn't that bad. What about the cushion I made for the church bazaar?'

'Mama finished it, as you know perfectly well.' Her face is pinched. She reminds me of my Latin teacher at school, the one I was scared of. 'The Miss Marion who says "I don't care if the hem of my tweed skirt is torn. I don't care if you don't like the company I keep. I'll make friends with whoever I want."'

She has a talent for mimicry, and I quite like the way she portrays me. I'm about to tell her that, but her movements are awkward and I see what's about to happen before she does.

'Careful!'

The cup is knocked over. Cold tea splashes over her lap. 'Now see what you've made me do!'

'Rather out of humour today, aren't you?'

'No thought for anyone but yourself.' She thrusts the stain in my face as she bustles out of the room. 'You know very well this tablecloth is for my bottom drawer.'

'Soak it in a solution of preservene soap.' I think I'm being helpful.

She turns back . I'm shocked by the hate in her face. 'Don't you ever, ever – you, of all people – tell me what to do!'

Amy and I look at one another. We hear air in the water pipes splutter from the kitchen tap.

'She's choking?'

Amy doesn't realise I'm joking. 'The water supply's low. Something to do with the pipes freezing, then thawing too quickly. There've been bursts everywhere. You were lucky, you know, to miss the worst of the weather.'

'Anyway, what's wrong with her? What did I say?'

'It's because Walter hasn't proposed yet. She expected him to, on her birthday.'

'He's bound to, eventually, isn't he?'

'I don't know.' She re-arranges daffodils in the vase. 'Don't you think, Marion, she might put a man off? She makes such a virtue of… being virtuous. You know what I mean? Always thinking of how to raise funds for this good cause or that good cause, always working on this committee or that committee.'

It's very seldom Amy voices opinions. 'Who've you been talking to, Amy?'

'And she's always talking about the children she's going to have, as if that's all that matters.'

Where she's standing, I can't see her face against the light.

'Marion… why didn't you marry Robert?'

I study the imprint of ink writing on the blotter. The measured and precise calligraphy is easily recognisable as papa's.

He usually writes at his own desk.

'When you had the chance? Everyone says he's so… such a gentleman, and fun too, and from a good family. I'd have liked him for a brother-in-law.'

The end of my cigarette taps 'gentleman' on the blotter: the very same rhythm as 'Tinker man'.

'You could've done very well out of it. You could've had a lovely home.'

'We're just friends.' I see that she knows something. 'How d'you know about me and Robert?'

'Some talk in town.'

I maintain a studied calm, exude only mild curiosity. 'What kind of talk?'

'You can't guess?'

I wonder if I should be worried. 'You haven't told me anything yet.'

'And they haven't – Robert and Margaret?'

'I don't know what you're talking about.'

'They're getting engaged.'

'Robert and Margaret?'

'That's what the news is. Not official though, not yet.' She studies my reaction. 'You don't mind?'

My laugh comes out as a cough, but it only takes a moment for me to recover. 'Of course I don't.'

'I thought maybe that was why papa sent you away – he'd heard and thought you might be upset.'

'Papa would never do something like that. Amy, can't you take things at face value? Aunt Tweedie is an elderly woman on her

own. She thought she'd some terrible illness. She wanted someone – family – to be with her.'

'Don't you mind even a little bit?'

'They would've told me if I'd been here.'

'But your two best friends?'

'We're all friends. It was a long time ago, Amy, and none of
your business.'

'Folk say you two were both... oh, I don't know... a bit different, maybe, from the rest of us.'

'I'm flattered, to be considered different.' A final draw on my
cigarette: 'But really, people shouldn't gossip.' I carry the ashtray
over to the fireplace to empty it before mama sees how many
cigarettes I've smoked.

'And perfect for one another. Then suddenly it was all over.'

'Robert and I have always been, and still are, good friends.'

'But you did love him, Marion, didn't you?'

'Ah, so that's it. Now we're getting to the point – you're in love?'

She's the first to look away. 'Well, actually, I... I think I may
be.'

'You'd know.'

'So you have been?'

'Enough of me. Tell me who it is, Amy. Come on, tell me!'
A weight has been lifted. I'm lightheaded: Mama will be so
delighted – Ethel and Amy both spoken for – that she'll hardly
notice I've gone. And Robert and Margaret... the saga comes to
a fitting end. Just Cissy... I wonder if she knows.

'Don't treat me like a child.'

'Then don't behave like one. Tell me who it is.'

'Well, I can't say yet… that's the problem. I'm not even sure. He may not be the right one.'

I should've been home before dark, but I like it better here, sitting on a log beside Nellie's campfire. The heat scalds my legs. Her big shawl is stretched across my back and wrapped round like a swaddling cloth. I'm daiving her to tell my fortune.

'*Yer mither wouldnae like it.*'

'*I willnae tell.*'

'*It costs ye siller.*'

'*Cissy tellt me it was a silver sixpence*'. *It sits in the middle of my upturned palm.*

'*Ach, yer haunds is ower cauld, lassie. Get some tea doon ye. I'll tell ye a story instead.*'

There's no arguing.

'*There was three lads want tae mairry this ae lassie. She says she'll tak the ane that brings her the finest present. The first brings gowd, the second the carcase o a deer. The third says he doesnae hae nae present but he'll tak her tae see a bonnie wee flower high up in the hills.*'

She pauses to blow the steam off her tea, stares at the fire.

Eventually I'm forced to ask. '*So…which ane did she marry?*'

'*Whit ane wuid you hae, lass?*'

'You've a choice, Amy?'

'Well, yes, of course.' She preens herself. 'But the one I'm thinking of… it certainly isn't what you think, Marion, he doesn't have a great deal of money. I suppose that's maybe a worry, as far as mama's concerned. And it's not what she might have hoped for. He isn't even the most handsome – but he's ambitious and single-minded and there's something about him I do like. I really do.'

'Has he said anything?'

She clears her throat. 'Not actually said. It's difficult. I think he's waiting for a sign from me. But, you know, from little things, I know he really likes me.'

I prod a tight muscle in my shoulder and wince.

'You spend far too much time at that desk. Here, let me.' Her hand kneads up my neck.

'That's sore.' She has a nice touch, gentle, but firm. Her hands must be stronger than they look.

'What can I do, Marion? I can't be sure yet. Maybe he thinks I'm too young. I need to know that he sees me, you know, in that special way, before I... I make myself clear.'

I allow myself to feel sisterly, and lace my fingers through her fingers. 'Here's an idea. Remember that old Tinker woman? The one that used to come to Arbroath?'

'Hair all over the place? You took me to her camp once when I was little. I was terrified.'

'She was harmless. Nellie, her name was. Anyway, she once told me a man falls in love with a woman's smell, not the way she looks. So all you've to do is tuck your hand in your armpit before you shake hands with him, and he'll never get you out of his mind.'

She takes her hand away. 'That's disgusting.'

Yawning and stretching, I meander over to the window:

spread my hands flat on the glass. The pane is so cold my hands almost stick to it. I peer to the right. A magpie on the top branch of the crab apple looks as if he's lost something.

'And no much wonder you're still on your own. Your hair stinks of cigarette smoke.'

No sign of him yet, but I'm not worried: if not today, tomorrow. 'The April sailin', was what he said. 'We'll aim for that.' I guess he'll be waiting under the tree when I open my bedroom curtains in the morning.

'Are you really, really sure?' I asked him.

'Fine that.'

He struggles to find words. And that makes every one precious.

I pick up my notebook and the thesaurus. I'm sure I can make room in the hatbox. Let me think: the clothes I'm taking are in the hold-all under the bed – the ones I'm leaving are pushed forward in the wardrobe to hide the gap behind. I'm carrying my jewellery in a velvet purse slung round my neck, my money in a pocket sewn into my underwear... so much to think about, and so little time left. What will I do about Margaret and Robert?

'Ethel's right about the company you keep!'

'What does she mean, the company I keep? Robert, Margaret?' I look beyond the blackbird, beyond the tree. Cissy, that's probably who she meant. She never liked Cissy. I've a – not just an idea, a flash of inspiration. Cissy won't know about Robert and Margaret, not yet, if it isn't official. I'll go to see her. We can laugh together... this is the excuse I've needed, the chance to put the past behind us.

'People like that old Tinker woman, I suppose.'

'It was the only advice I could think of, Amy.'

'Well, thank you very much for nothing.'

'Excuse me, dear, there's something I absolutely must finish.' I sit back at the desk and dip my pen in the inkwell. Two short sentences later, I'm ready. That'll do it. Perfect. I'll hand it in on my way to see Cissy.

PART II

CHAPTER 7

⌒

Glasgow: May, 1930

I don't recognise the woman, don't know anyone in the wee group around her. It might be someone else she's waving to.

A glance behind says it's me.

She's beckoning. If I heard her speak I'd remember… but she may just have mistaken me for someone else. My gesture to the far side of the room is ridiculously exaggerated, but I convince myself I look as if I know exactly where I'm going and who I'm going to meet.

Good… she's turning back to her friends.

There's such a buzz of conversation it's impossible to make out anything that's being said. I push my way through the crowd, happy to be invisible. But, just in case someone spots me, I hold the smile. My face hurts.

Thank God: a wee space for me – a wall behind my back and a bay window– even if it is just a view of the street below. I wipe the palms of my hands on my skirt. No-one notices.

There's a hullaballoo going on at the corner of the street. Cars are trying to pass a broken-down cart – in both directions, I realise. Traffic outside the hotel is almost at a standstill. I hope it doesn't delay proceedings too much.

I'd hate to queue morning and night, every day. But at least the people at the bus stop have something to watch until their bus comes. They're bound to be late home though… I do hope Ethel isn't worrying about me.

My reflection in the glass startles me for a moment. I used to like this dress, but it was fashionable then and fitted better. I reach out as I'd reach to touch a ghost. Are you really there? Or to someone in need of comfort… but stop myself in time.

Everyone's caught up in their own affairs. No-one has noticed. I must go home tomorrow.

That young woman stepping from the taxi – it's that young novelist, isn't it? The one who lives in Glasgow. Her name will come back to me in a minute. Two young men are falling over themselves for her attention… the air around charged with energy.

In Europe, that first time – I was hardly more than a girl – that was when I came alive… under those great mountain peaks striking to the sky.

A crowd of us take the steamer across the lake to the weekly market at Vevey. It's spring and the air is sweet with the scent of almond blossom. Children chase each other round the pillars of the old market building, pigeons flutter under its roof and sun themselves on wide, shallow steps. The old clock in its belfry rings the hours.

There's hardly room to walk between great piles of lettuce, asparagus, endive; vegetables we've never seen before; wallflower, daffodils and lilac. One stall sells nothing but violets, another lilies. Robert says lilies glory in their sex – an unconcealed array, an unashamed shower of golden dust. He chooses lilies for me. I make such a fuss over them he buys more. I laugh. He buys more, and more, and more. It's difficult to hold them all. I lift the front of my skirt and fill it.

The locals are indulgent with foreigners.

When the others climb up to see the old church we hide behind two pillars of the old market building. Later we follow a path by the lake. I float lily flowers on the water, give a bunch to an old woman. The basket on her back is loaded with firewood. A man leaning over a window ledge calls to us to taste his new wine. It's effervescent and sweet and exhilarating.

Later still, when the moon's low, tinged with red, not pale like at home, we swim along its path in the ice-cold water. Even though the lake is calm, black and silent, there's a strong current below the surface. We watch the lights of the steamer in the distance as it makes its way back without us.

'How do you do.'

It's the man from the BBC, and he's holding out his hand. I manage the formalities perfectly well.

He's sorry he wasn't available to talk the other day. It's always better to make an appointment.

It's of no consequence. I happened to be passing – took a chance to thank his staff again, for putting me at such ease!

A lady wrote in to say how much she enjoyed my talk.

How kind of her.

He didn't expect to see me here.

He surely can't mean… no, there's nothing in his expression to suggest he's read the article.

A copy of the letter – very charming letter – is on its way to Aberdeen.

As I thank him profusely, I'm weighing things up. This isn't the best place. I ought to wait, perhaps write after I get home, but on the other hand…

Given the great potential of the wireless for promoting poetry, I wonder whether he has considered… would he be interested in a proposal for a series of programmes on the importance of 'place' in Scottish poetry? I don't give him the chance to say anything at that point, just launch into explanation and justification.

Well, of course, he's always on the lookout for ideas…

Would he like to read a script?

I might not appreciate the amount of work involved in such an undertaking.

I've done the research, the planning: know the thrust of the argument, drawn up outlines of what each programme might cover. My voice wavers on the indignant.

Audiences tend to like variety. The corporation doesn't normally commission a whole series at one time, not using the same writer… or the same presenter.

I remind him of some examples. His eyes glaze over.

It has been done, of course, where the series was likely to have wide appeal. But he has to consider every angle… there might be a more limited audience… now if a more well-known poet were to…

He tries to look down on me, but I'm as tall as he is.

I learned a lot from papa, and can still draw it out of the hat on occasion. The anger that makes me quiver sharpens my wit and my resolve. I speak with subtlety and charm.

He's not sure whether I'm being sarcastic, whether to take offence, or whether he has just lost a great opportunity: hardly knows how to respond, and doesn't like that. It gives me some satisfaction to watch him squirm, even if my chances of future work with the BBC are as dust under a carpet. He searches faces in the crowd and excuses himself, having spied someone he must talk to.

I'm worn out, but it's safe here at the window: I can look out or watch the crowd as I please. The lady who waved… there's the look of Edinburgh about her. Yes! We were introduced at a poetry evening. That's all, nothing more than that. She asked if I'd look at some of her poems, and perhaps might advise her, if I thought they were any good.

I choose the Amontillado when a waiter offers a choice of sherry.

The crowd surges like a tide, in time to music, one might almost suspect. But, actually, it's nothing to do with the the pianist in the far corner. It's the man himself, the saviour of Scottish poetry, who's made his usual – larger than life – entry, sucking the crowd into his magnetic field. But it's not just Mr Grieve – or whatever it is he chooses to call himself now – and his entourage. Everyone else seems so well acquainted.

My reflection looks lonely, my clothes quaint. No wonder people think my ideas… I should probably go straight home tomorrow.

The big double doors to the dining room are being opened. Oh dear… long tables. I send up a prayer. Let me find someone soon, someone I know, to sit with. A woman, from the northeast… Nan, preferably, though I've seen no sign of her yet.

Someone comes from behind, touches me on the shoulder. 'Marion!'

'Miss Cruik… Helen!'

'I'm so pleased you're here.'

'Yes, I thought it best to warn you I might not be able to come, but…'

'Your sister is better?'

'Yes. Well, here I am.'

'I hoped you'd change your mind. That's why I kept your name on the guest list.'

'Thank you so much. It's such an honour… to be here. No, really, I mean it! Amongst all these literary people!'

'We'd an excellent response, I must say.'

'I didn't expect such a big company.'

She leans close. 'I let the word out that the Edinburgh clique were coming in force, and the Glasgow people didn't want to be outdone.'

'And from the north?'

'A few… yes. By the way, I did the table plans. I've put you next to Miss Shepherd.'

'Well, it wouldn't have mattered, of course, with so many like-minded people, but I did hope to see her here.'

'You didn't come down together, then?'

'Actually, I've been in Glasgow for a few days already – staying with my other sister and her husband – visiting friends, paying back a day here, a day there, trying to cram everyone in.'

'And are you well enough?' Only when I feel the grip of her hand do I realise how cold mine are.

'No, I'm fine. It's just the effort… you know, trains and buses – getting to appointments on time. And when you haven't seen people for a while… going over the same things again and again.'

'Your writing?'

'I fitted in a little business.'

'You must keep at it, you know. No-one will push if you don't. You could even make some new contacts tonight, if you tried. Anyone who is anyone, in publishing, is here.'

'But Helen… you know, I'm not good at that sort of thing. And you'll have seen it – the article?'

'Don't give it another thought, my dear. He's a genius, of course, and has such energy! But… 'vitriolic' is too kind a word! He can be a very prickly thistle. You know what he's like, always has to be slanging somebody!'

'Yet, when I first met him…'

She puts a finger to her lips. It's difficult to make out the announcement, but from the general movement I gather we're summoned to the dining room. She points to where the crowd is most dense. 'Excuse me, dear, I'll have to rescue the guest speaker from our mutual friend.'

Staff clear the debris from our table, leaving only the dainty floral arrangements down the centre, a stain of chicken gravy and someone's spilt red wine. Amongst the chatter, there's an occasional scraping of chair legs as someone leaves to catch an early bus or train.

Blood is pulsing in my temples. I'll never get to sleep tonight, not after this, but every second I'll lie awake will be worth it.

Mr Mitchell catches my eye again, even though he's across the table and three places down. I can't quite hear what he's saying but gather he's remembered another story about the minister from Logie Pert. I take my cue from his gesticulations and think I laugh at the appropriate times.

A mass exodus of those catching the last train to Edinburgh, Helen among them. I agree to visit next time I'm in the capital. Mr Gunn comes over to say goodbye and what a pleasure it was. He hopes we meet again. His handshake is firm, his tone earnest. He leans forward to speak in my ear. If my work is 'parochial' he's happy for his to be described in the very same way. For him to say that – him of all people, whom I so admire – to be so kind. I'm not able to say anything, but my silence is of no consequence. He knows the effect his words have on me.

Nan walks with me to collect my coat, fusses over me, waits with me at reception until Walter arrives. With her hair up she's so sophisticated. I feel like an old aunt from the country.

'You look tired, dear.' she says.

'But it's been such a lovely evening.'

'I haven't asked about your sister.'

'She's well, thank you. I left her with my mind at ease. It's just… she has such a delicate constitution. That's the problem. So she catches everything that's going! But now the winter's over…'

'And the situation… that you mentioned?'

I check who's around.

'I don't mean to pry.'

'I am anxious to get some little jobs. But with my lectures… Glasgow women graduates this week, one in Edinburgh coming up – the annual Women's Guild meeting. Then on the first Thursday of next month, my talk in Aberdeen, and an article to finish for the Scots Observer.'

'And your poetry?'

'The Porpoise Press want a collection.'

'New work?'

'Well, finding time will be difficult.'

'You're writing articles, though.'

'I can't concentrate on poetry. Not at the moment, not now. But yes, an article. There's one I'm working on.'

'You mustn't take such criticism to heart. That was only one point of view. Look at the number of critics who value your work.'

'No, really, it's not that. It's just I'm a little tired. I think I'd a touch of flu myself.'

'You're doing far too much, for too little return. And the problem is, things are so difficult generally.'

'Money doesn't go far these days.' I rearrange the edges of my bolero so it doesn't sag.

'And the slump is getting worse, I fear.'

'I never did understand stocks and shares, to be honest. I didn't have to. One must trust one's banker, don't you agree? In my case, his father was a friend of my father, so I'm sure none of it is his fault.'

'Radio work, remember, I suggested. If you can get it, that pays better.'

'Yes, but…'

'I know, it's a little world full of intrigues and jealousies.'

'Anyway, I've hardly the time to write a letter.'

'But you'll make time for walking? One day soon we might get back on these little hill tracks above Dinnet.'

Just the two of us, I hope. With the wind in our backs, her golden hair blowing over her shoulders, she looks like a wood nymph.

CHAPTER 8

Aberdeen: May 1930

The mattress remembers my shape. My breathing's slow and even. I drift, semi-conscious. Everything's lightsome.

A clatter from the kitchen: I pull the quilt over my ears. It settles round my shoulders, soft and warm. Rings of light pulse and blur and merge on my eyelids.

Her shoes clip on the stairs. My bedroom door bangs against the side of the wardrobe, making the hangers rattle. A teaspoon slides round a saucer as the tray's set down.

She didn't knock.

'Marion.' She knows I'm awake.

If I move now, just stretch a little bit, it'll be all right. The moment passes.

'Marion?' last syllable stressed – tone rising: her 'enough-of-this-nonsense' voice. One hand will be twisting the lock of hair behind her ear.

The dim light of a very early morning: Amy's crying again and mama's walking the floor.

A loud whisper: 'Marion.'

It's Ethel's little hand that's grasping and pulling at the sleeve of my nightgown.

'Go back to bed.'

'That's what mama said.'

'What do you want?'

'The baby woke me.'

'She'll settle soon.'

'It's not fair.'

'What's not fair?'

She lifts my hand and bares her teeth and guides my finger into her mouth. Her teeth gleam like river pearls. 'My tooth was there when I went to bed, but when I woke up it'd gone.'

'It'll be under your pillow.'

Her wail a fair copy of the real thing, but from the wrong place. 'I swallowed it.'

A sharp point's poking through the gum. 'There's another tooth coming.'

'I don't want a new one. I want that one.'

I lift the covers. She slips in beside me.

'All right. In you come.' My arms wrap all the way round her and more. She snuggles in close. My hand encloses both of hers. Her hair smells of lavender water, her feet are cold between my thighs.

A prod on the shoulder.

I stir, sit up on one elbow, attempt a yawn that comes out as a sigh. 'Ethel! What time is it?' My mouth has learned the shape of mama's smile.

'Thought you were never going to waken.'

I'm taken aback by her clothes, then realise it's Sunday and she's ready for church. Her hair's pulled flat against her head: just that one loose strand she can't control.

The curtains are yanked open so hard I fear they'll come off the rail. Sunlight bursts into the room. My eyes hurt.

She's thrusting the tray at me. 'I've brought your breakfast.'

I fix the pillow behind my back and pull myself into a sitting position. My knees come up to support the tray.

'Didn't think you'd want much.' She folds her arms, stands back.

'This is perfect. Thank you.'

'My little "welcome home" – if you like.' She waits.

I stir the tea.

'Since I was in bed when you got back.'

Hard to tell her mood from the tone of her voice: it's probably nothing. 'Yes, sorry to be late.'

'Rather expected you on the earlier train.' She opens my wardrobe door, makes a show of brushing dust from the lapel of my suit. 'I know you wouldn't say which one you'd get but… anyway, I ironed your blouse for this morning.'

'You didn't have to do that, dear.'

'I don't expect you'd have done it:' the jocular tone that isn't.

I don't need to get into an argument, not so soon, not after yesterday.

'Toast all right, is it? Not too cold?'

It's hard to swallow when she's watching. 'Lovely, thank you.'

She tuts at the sight of the dress I took off last night lying across the back of my bedside chair. It's lifted, shaken down and only when she's satisfied I've noticed, is it hung up. The seat of the chair is dusted down with an open hand. She perches on the edge.

'Tell me about it, then. Did you have a good time?'

The speech I rehearsed on the train comes into my head. I nibble at the crust of the toast. 'Such a treat... breakfast in bed! I didn't expect this!' Better she doesn't suspect anything, not even that I enjoyed the slightest part of it. I make a calculated switch to business-like, trawl my brain for what might be acceptable. 'Very busy. Tiresome meetings and duty visits, most of them quite routine. Nothing remotely exciting.' I'm smiling too much and talking too much and we both know I'm trying too hard.

The photograph of papa that was taken not long before he died, the one on my dressing table, is picked up and scrutinised minutely.

'I find it very difficult, I must admit. You know, if I could just write poetry...'

'"If I could just write poetry..." Just listen to yourself, complaining again.'

'I don't mean it like that, Ethel. Not at home. I'm happy to do my share of the chores.'

'When you're here.'

I choose to ignore the remark, grope for words that might

engage her in conversation. 'It's this… this literary business, Ethel… not the writing poetry, it's the publishing side of things. I struggle sometimes, I really do. Things are never straight-forward… like, for example, "by the way, whose copyright is it?" You know, you'd think if it's my poetry… nobody's saying it isn't my poetry, but it's beyond me, that's the truth, this copyright business. And literary meetings. You have to go, but believe me, polite conversation is so tiring when people actually aren't interested in you at all, not as a person, just hope you can open some door for them. Which I most obviously cannot do.'

'But, Marion.' My hand-mirror, comb and brush get arranged in parallel lines. 'All I wanted to know was, did you have any success?'

'Some people ask you to give a lecture then think they're doing you a favour if they pay no more than travelling expenses.'

'Success, Marion?'

'Nothing definite.'

The extent of my failure is defined by a spread of fingers. 'Total waste of time?'

A warning flutter in my chest: 'Not entirely, dear. I met some-one from the BBC. We'd an interesting chat. Something might come from that. And I started a new poem, on the way home, for the new collection. You know, the one I told you about?' I don't let her interrupt. 'The train stopped at Lunan. It was dark by then of course, just the moonlight on the bay. But it remind-ed me of when we were young. Remember the fun we used to have at Lunan? When we were little? You loved playing in the dunes, creating your own little worlds.' I run out of steam.

If she remembers she doesn't want me to know. 'I suppose "The BBC" will mean another trip to Glasgow.'

'Well, perhaps, if anything comes of it. Of course I can't guarantee that, not yet.'

'Well then, not a lot to show for five days away and a train fare we can ill afford.' She stands with her back to the window.

'I told you, Ethel, the university did pay my travel costs. That was why I was able to go. The other things just fitted around. And I stayed with Amy, so it wasn't as if I'd any accommodation expenses.'

'Oh, well then. All right for some. What about your trip to Arbroath? I suppose that was a pleasant enough sojourn?'

'Pleasant enough, though another duty visit.'

'Are they well?'

'Margaret's much better. But if it hadn't been for her house-keeper... she's been a gem, Margaret says, while she was ill.'

'A local girl?'

'Yes, actually.'

'Someone we know?'

'Remember the Greigs?' She shakes her head.

'Cissy Greig? She was in the same class as me.'

'Those Greigs?' – the face she'd put on if she found something foustie in the bread bin. 'Your little friend.'

'Don't be like that, Ethel. Cissy and I were good friends, for a while.'

'James Street, wasn't it, they lived?'

Her expression is worrying me. 'Anyway, it's Cissy's daughter – Minnie.'

'You were called Minnie when you were little.'

Mama leaves with the baby.

'Shush,' I say. 'Don't cry. Do you want to see something?'

The snowglobe's on my bookshelf. I take it down, crouch so her eyes are at the right level. They widen when she sees the tiny castle inside.

'What is it, Minnie?'

I shake hard.

She's mesmerised by the swirling snowflakes. She wants to take the globe from me.

'No, Ethel,' I say. 'It's too heavy for you.'

I lift her up on my lap. Her little hands don't go all the way round but if I put my hands over hers… we shake it together.

Her nose is pressed against the glass.

'What is it?' she asks again.

'It's magic.'

'Can we go there, Minnie? You and me? Can we?'

'You used to call me Minnie. Well, anyway, Cissy died when her daughter was about sixteen – no, Ethel, I didn't know about it. Why would I? Last time I saw Cissy was years ago, probably before papa died. Anyway, eventually someone at the kirk asked Margaret and Robert to take the girl in and train her. I must say it's turned out very well, with Robert being away so much. The girl has made herself quite indispensable. And the fact they've no children of their own…'

Ethel's hands clasp behind her, pulling her shoulders back.

'I didn't mean to bore you. They send their best regards, by the way, Robert and Margaret.'

She gestures. 'I'll take the tray, then, shall I?'

A triangle of toast left, but I don't want it. 'Thank you so much, that was delicious.'

She leans over to lift the tray from my knees. It's such an ordinary thing to do, and done so naturally, that, just for a second, I forget there's anything wrong.

'Ethel, I don't think I'll come to the service today.' I hear the ticking of the clock.

'I haven't been out since you left.'

'But, dear, you can go by yourself.'

A hiss. 'I can't.'

'I'm really tired…'

'Tired? You've just wakened. I've been up for hours. Done the housework – nothing left for you to do. At all.'

'It's just with being on the go all last week, and sitting on the train – my ankles are swollen.'

'Oh you poor darling!'

I'm not taken in.

'Don't tell me! Amy didn't bring you breakfast in bed once! Oh, shame!' The tray thumps down on the dressing table. 'How silly of me not to realise. And what an ordeal… he took you to the station, did he? All the way from Greenock to Glasgow, in the new car – that must have been so tiring!'

I tell myself not to interrupt. Let it wash over. Please God, it will wash over. Please God…

Papa comes down to the level of the congregation. A hush in the kirk... not a rustle, not a cough. We all wait. He raises his arm, makes the sign with his fingers.

'... and may the blessing of God Almighty, Father, Son and Holy Ghost, rest on and abide with you, now and ever more'.

I breathe his voice in, and out, in, and out, in, and out. It calms me: usually does.

She's still speaking. 'Tired from having a stop off in Arbroath – tea with friends? Out walking on the cliffs? I'll bet you fitted that in. Some of us haven't been back to Arbroath for years, you know – but then, you never think of that do you?'

'Ethel, dearest...' I stretch my hand out but she won't look me in the eye. I'm afraid I can't do this much longer.

'And not so much as a "Sorry I was late home, Ethel Mary", or "Thank you, Ethel Mary, I knew you'd have supper waiting for me."'

It makes her worse if I show any weakness. I try to pull myself together but there's a pain in my lower back and... I can't think what else to say or do. There's no way I can make it right. 'I'm sorry, Ethel.'

'Look at you. And not even "I hope you kept well, Ethel Mary, while I was away?" '

'Did you keep well? I didn't mean to be selfish.' I feel silly smiling as I wipe my eyes on the sheet before I push it aside. My ankles are twice the size they should be. 'There, look, my legs are much better for a night's rest. I'll get up and go with you. The exercise will do me good.'

'You're pathetic.' Her breathing's very shallow.

'Just give me a few minutes, dear?'

'You're trying to humour me.'

'No. I've decided. It's a beautiful day. I'll come. All I'm worried about…' I started and there's no escape. 'It's just… are you sure you're feeling well enough, today, dear?' I make a show of folding back the quilt. 'A walk in the hills, perhaps, instead? This afternoon? You'd like that, wouldn't you?'

She brushes her hand across the desk, scattering my things on the floor.

'Ethel, dear…'

'Don't "Ethel, dear" me! My name's Ethel Mary.' She paces the room. 'You entice me to this… this godforsaken place to live, and if you're not scratching with your pen you're rushing off to town or you "must" go to this meeting, "Ethel dear", or that meeting, "Ethel dear," or "I've been invited to give a lecture, Ethel dear" – as if I care – or "so and so's invited me out to lunch, Ethel dear" – I wouldn't come, even if you did ask me. All you talk about is poets – dead poets mostly.'

'Don't get so upset, darling.' My voice shakier than I want it to be: 'I didn't mean any harm.'

'Who says I'm upset? "I must see my publisher today, Ethel dear"; "I've a committee meeting in Glasgow, Ethel dear"; "I'll stay with Amy for a few days, Ethel dear – poor Amy isn't well at all, Ethel dear."'

She's shouting, and that's maybe good. The storm may blow itself out.

'If it brought in any money, that might be different. I could understand, perhaps.' She kicks my notebook. 'Poetry this and poetry that and poetry the next thing. Poetry, poetry, poetry. All you care about.'

'That's not fair. And not true, Ethel Mary.' I swing my legs out of bed, but they're unsteady and I almost lose my balance. I grab her for support.

'Leave me alone! "Not true, Ethel Mary." Well, that's what it looks like from here. And if it isn't poetry it's Margaret's bad back or Amy's… imaginary whatever it is. As if we hadn't all been through that already.'

'It isn't imaginary. If you saw her, you couldn't help but be sorry. All these years and she's never given up hope, not until now.' Determined now to get things back under control, I link my arm in her arm.

'She's not the only woman who wanted children.'

'I know that.'

'So wrapped up in herself she never thinks of anyone else. Never has done. Never will.'

'There, there.'

'Neither of you do. You say you want a companion and then you go gallivanting all over the country and leave me behind. You don't want a companion. You want a… a housekeeper – so you can be upsides with Margaret Cunningham.'

Miss Williamina Greig, housekeeper. Minnie Greig. I've rehearsed it so often, it should be easy. 'Minnie is my dear friend,' I want to say, 'my very dear friend. It's Minnie I go to see, when I get the chance. Not Margaret, not Robert. She's young and bright, interesting… and makes me laugh! When did you ever see me laugh, Ethel?'

She's waiting for a reaction.

I ask if she's taken her pills yet.

'Why would you care?'

'Of course I do.'

'Don't make me laugh. Don't pretend.' She shrugs my arm away. 'All you care about is that I pay my share of the expenses.'

'Shall I fetch your pills?'

'You think I'm a child?'

'Of course not.'

'I'm fifty-four, for Heaven's sake. I'm not a little sister any more.' I nod. 'I've seen things you've never dreamed of. You've forgotten that, haven't you?' My head still nods, though I wonder whether it should be shaking. 'And what did you do in the war?'

Nothing to say, no answer to give.

'Write poetry? Make scones? And you think you can tell me what to do?'

'I know what you did. It must have been a terrible experience.'

'You don't understand, at all, do you? And why would you, living in a fantasy world?' The way her face twists scares me. 'Terrible? What would you know? Soldiers – real, brave men, not figments of my imagination – needed me. Needed.' She punches her own chest with two fingers. 'Me. What's terrible about that?'

'But for someone as sensitive…'

'"Would anyone like some tea and scones?" Is that what you said? Dear God, Marion, you never could bake, not even scones.'

'If I'd been younger, I might have done something worthwhile.'

'Who ever needed you? My soldiers appreciated every touch, every word.' Her chin points up a little.

'Papa would've been so proud of you.'

'And now I'm on my own, day after day... no-one to talk to. You're always stuck in your room, even if you're at home.'

'But Ethel... you usually say you like being on your own.'

'I say what?'

'You like peace to listen to music on the wireless. And you don't like being interrupted when you're sewing.'

'Sewing! "Lady, skilled in alterations and mending." You call that "sewing"?'

No point in asking her to keep her voice down.

'Mother'd turn in her grave if she knew. And you could so easily get a proper job.'

'What if you were to get back in touch with some of the nurses you used to know?'

'What for?'

'You could invite them for tea.'

'Why?'

'Or to stay.'

'Here? Are you serious? We've hardly enough to live on.'

I hear the couple from next-door in their garden, reach out to close the window but can't stretch far enough.

'You said we'd have enough. More fool me to believe you.'

'It's not my fault, Ethel. It's happening all over, people losing money. Lots of people are having to make do. We haven't done too badly, really, not yet.'

'Well I've had enough. I'm sick. Sick!' She stomps towards the door. 'Sick of living here. Sick of having nothing and no-one. Sick of you and your poetry.'

At least she doesn't fall this time, though she takes the stairs two at a time.

I try to find the sleeves of my dressing gown.

Even though I'm half expecting it, the din in the kitchen comes as a shock. I cover my ears but that doesn't shut it out... a lull and if I'm lucky that'll be it.

It starts again, the doors of the cupboards banging in turn. Less fiercely, I think, this time, more of a rhythm and I hope that means she's coming round.

A different sound: a dull thud. I'm at the foot of the stairs. As I go into the kitchen there's another. I throw myself between her head and the wall. 'No Ethel!'

'Sick! Sick!'

Everything's hurting, not just where she punches and kicks me, but I manage to hold on. I can't let go, not yet. We fall to the floor – a chair's knocked over. I pin her wrists and cover her body with mine. My weight – for all it is – keeps her down. I just have to endure...

Ever earnest Ethel-Mary endures...
Emergency... emergency

She's cursing, but doesn't really mean it. She'd never say these things if she was well. From this angle I see a crossbar on the stool has broken.

I ease one hand away to stroke her hair away from her forehead, but change my mind. Not yet. My own hair has fallen
over my face. At last – five minutes? Longer maybe, I've no idea
– she's quiet.

'Let me go, Marion.'

I ease back. A bruise on her forehead, and one on her cheek-
bone's spreading fast. There's the slightest pinpoint of light in
her eyes. I sit back on my heels.

That's it. Over. Not too much harm. A cold compress on the
bruises, a cup of sweet tea. I think I say 'It's all right, dear,' but
I'm not sure if I say it aloud. I reach for the kitchen table to pull
myself up. My hand pressed against the table-top, I help Ethel
to her feet.

The bread knife's still lying where she sliced my toast. I watch
her pick it up. I watch it make an arc through the air and pin the
joint of my finger to the table. I don't feel anything, just wonder
why the cut edges of flesh turn inwards. It doesn't bleed, not
immediately, not even when she pulls the point of the knife out
again.

There's a knock at the door.

If we're quiet, they'll go away. They mean well, but Ethel will
be fine now, if we're left alone.

She sinks to the floor, sobbing, clutching my legs. 'I'm sorry,
Marion. I didn't mean it. You know I didn't mean it.'

There's a pattern of shifting light on the wall.

'Look, Ethel!'

She lifts her eyes.

'Don't you see? The way it moves. Isn't it pretty.' The angle of the northern sun does it, this time of year, this time of day, glancing off the river.

The hammering on the door is louder. It's kind of them to take the trouble... my tongue's sticking to the roof of my mouth.

There's the lavatory, just behind me, beside the front door. I could go there, bolt the door and stand with my back against it. There's room enough.

A red flow across my palm. 'It's all right, dear. It's nothing.' I hold the edges of the wound together with my teeth. The blood's warm, the taste not unpleasant.

Ethel's face is hard against my knees. How could I ever have thought of leaving her?

Hairpins are sticking out from her hair. With my good hand I push it back, replace some of the pins so she'll look smart.

CHAPTER 9

☙

Glasgow: May, 1930

There's a place I go to, sometimes.

Wide open moorland: I'm on a hilltrack, walking in such perfect balance my feet hardly touch the ground.

The two men in front of me jump from the platform before the bus has stopped. A woman elbows me aside. I grab the rail to steady myself. The conductor's standing with his finger on the bell, but it's not easy, such a deep step, my knees the way they are, and my bag, and the umbrella and the parcel from Amy, so awkward to carry.

A moment to take my bearings... the flow of the crowd will be towards the centre of town at this time of day. I turn the opposite way, and there's my first landmark – the hotel Walter mentioned, on the other side of the street.

Three of us are waiting to cross the road. One's a nurse: a cape is so very practical in this weather. I wonder if she's going to work and think it'd do no harm to say, 'Good afternoon' and ask if I can walk with her. But whether it's the place or the rain or the way she looks, or whether it's my age, my mood... I don't. I say, to no-one in particular – and no-one takes any notice – that at least the rain's in our back. A gap opens up in the traffic. I'm carried over the road by a press of people. Something has been spilt in the gutter at the far side, but I wade through it, so I don't lose sight of the nurse.

We take the next side road after the hotel, and suddenly there are trees along the pavement and the traffic noise seems far away. I could stop here to put my brolly up but decide it's not worth the effort. My coat chafes the calves of my legs. The rim of my hat presses against my forehead, and I think I'd be more comfortable without the gloves.

Two weeks since Walter collected us. Two weeks of constant rain. How can Amy bear to live here? To make things worse, nothing ever dries: the manse is so damp. I keep my head down.

We've arrived at the back of the hospital... the nurse disappears into a staff entrance. Water overflows from guttering. When I turn one corner, then another, I recognise the facade and the main entrance. My back against the swing door pushes it: I squelch my way inside. A cleaner wields a mop in an attempt to keep the floor dry.

I didn't realise how high the ceiling was, last time.

The door shudders again, spills out another visitor, one who knows to report to the woman behind the reception window. I wait as he goes through the process then step forward. I don't understand the receptionist and she doesn't understand my accent. The lady behind me digs me in the ribs. 'It's just a form to be filled in.'

I get through by reading it upside down: name, relationship to patient; patient's name, category and ward; responsible psychiatrist, authorisation. The receptionist points to the stairs and explains how to get to the day-room.

I hesitate.

The cleaner is summoned to show the way. A bunch of keys hangs low from her belt. She walks like a man, feet splayed out. Robert used to tramp like that, as if walking was a serious business. Wull had a way of dancing on the balls of his feet.

I apologise for the marks my wet shoes are making on the clean floor. She doesn't speak.

It's dry and warm in the corridors, and surprisingly peaceful, though I hear a distant hue and cry behind one of the heavy doors. The smell of the wood panelling reminds me of home, on a Friday, when I was a child, and the furniture was polished. In different circumstances I'd stop to look at the paintings on the walls, but I get the feeling no-one ever does.

The door of the day-room (PRIVATE PATIENTS) doesn't need a key. It's brighter than I expect – there was a hotel in Brussels, Margaret and I stayed in once: the salon was much like this. Chairs, armchairs, occasional tables placed in groups, murmured conversations... you imagine little intrigues. Monsieur Renard waited for us there, the night he took us to the opera.

People look up when I enter, but don't stare. Women – and men – are sitting by themselves or in groups...a woman nearby reading a book, a man in the corner with a newspaper spread out on the table. One woman knits, some sew, two men are bent over an octagonal chess table. Ethel's by herself, sitting beside a window. Her hair's down, softer round her face. Her needle's busy.

The forward lean of her frame, the angle of the neck, the profile – the pointed chin, remind me of mama. The way she has her ankles crossed, legs tucked back, embroidery neat on her lap: it could be mama.

'Ethel!'

She checks her stitches.

She probably didn't even expect me today. And what with the constant rattle of the wind throwing rain at the window-panes... the rhythm of it would make you... it's almost hypnotic.

She starts sewing again, but the way she's yarking at the thread, I think she did hear me.

'Ethel?' Because I don't want to raise my voice, I rest my hand on her shoulder.

She looks at my hand.

I kiss her cheek. 'Ethel, dear.'

Her needle is still poised for the next stitch. Her gaze goes beyond me.

I set my bag and the parcel from Amy on the floor.

'Sorry, dear, I'm soaked through. You can't imagine...' My mouth dries up. I stifle a cough that isn't there but even that doesn't give me time to think of a different way to end the sentence: 'how awful it is out there.'

No reaction.

'I'll hang my coat up, shall I?'

There's a coat-stand near the door. When I come back she's finishing off a thread at the back of her work.

'Shall I pull this chair over?'

She selects a deep yellow yarn, rethreads the needle.

'A new sampler you're working on?' I lean over but the embroidery is in a frame. I can't make out the writing.

Only her hand moves.

'I'm so pleased to see you looking well, Ethel. You are well, aren't you? And your room? Is it comfortable? We do so want you to be comfortable.'

The tobacco smoke in the room makes me crave a cigarette, but I daren't, not the way my chest has been.

'You've certainly been busy in the last fortnight! Your embroidery's coming on very well.'

I didn't notice the piano when I came in first. If there was a pianist as well, it'd be even more like that salon in Brussels.

I move my chair nearer. 'You've chosen such lovely colours.'

She looks up as another visitor comes through the door.

The man's eyes flit from one group to another, rest briefly on mine. I realise it might not be easy to distinguish between guests and patients. 'Do tell me how you've settled in?' – my voice louder than it should be.

The very heavy rain eases. I can see into the grounds now, recognise the colour of larch trees, the shape of a horse chestnut. There's another public building on the skyline – with a spire or a clock tower. My eyesight's not good enough to tell the difference any more.

I wonder aloud if the sky's beginning to lift.

'And Walter?' She doesn't even look up.

The weight in my chest reminds me it's not going anywhere.

'Amy?'

'Of course. Here, look what she sent! Some personal things.' I point at the parcel then remember the letter, and scrabble about in my handbag. 'They both send their love – lots of love – and every good wish.' I don't say she's constantly in their prayers.

Her needle's going at speed. 'Not coming, then.'

I tell her how sorry Amy was: she's not well, her nerves are bad. I say it can't be healthy living so close to the river – what with the rain never stopping. And by the way, lots of other people are asking for her. I reel off some names. And did she get a letter from cousin John in Aberdeen? He said he'd write. Is there anyone she'd like me to... let them know? Would she like notepaper? And was she remembering about the cottage on Skye? I tell her the lady was most understanding when I cancelled the booking.

She looks up.

'Of course I didn't give out any personal details, just said there was illness in the family. But we can go another time, Ethel. Only I've been thinking, as it's so wet on this side of the country, perhaps we should go south instead?'

The muscles of her face twitch. The moment passes.

If I could pace the room, that'd keep me calm. But all those people...

Tearful, but not complaining, she was, when we brought her. I suppose, in a way, she respects hospitals. And Walter's used to dealing with people in crises. She'd walk naked up Sauchiehall Street, if he asked her to. That the doctor was Walter's friend made a huge difference. And give the man his due, he gave quite a performance, soothing and charming in equal measure. His talk of 'assessment' and 'recuperation' was convincing. It was amazing how 'nervous' patients could be put right, he said, sometimes in no time at all. What with her willingness to come in on a voluntary basis... that always made a difference, showed the patient wanted to be well. It was how they, in the hospital, liked to work. And of course the staff were trained in modern methods and had access to the best medicines.

It wasn't at all the ordeal I expected. Nothing like as bad as this. What would I not give, for her to speak? Please God.

In the grounds I notice a clump of tall beech trees, the leaves on the branches still pale and fresh against the grey bark.

'You'll ruin your scarf twisting it like that.'

She's right. The weave is opening up. But the fringe is frayed too, with age. 'Aunt Tweedie gave it to me when I was quite a little girl.'

'You should look after it then.'

'D'you remember, Ethel? The summer Aunt Tweedie came to help mama? Just after George was born?'

Nothing said, but a flicker of reaction.

'Amy was still a baby. Aunt Tweedie looked after her. And mama was so tired, she never came out of her room. They said I was old enough to look after you. Remember? Playing in the dens with Cissy and me? And we took you to Carlinhaugh with her little brothers. Remember the rockpools?'

She doesn't admit to anything.

'You wouldn't come into the cave, though.'

A raised voice across the room unlocks something.

'The Colonel,' she says.

I'm taken aback. 'A military man?'

That makes her smirk. 'Most colonels are.'

'Not someone you know though?'

She inclines her head just enough to indicate she may know him.

She never could tell a lie, not the way I could.

I follow the movement of clouds across the sky and hope the wind will blow them all away. 'It was lovely, wasn't it, Ethel, when we moved into our little house, when you came home from the war.'

'You were always in your room.'

'But to have someone there, you know, when we wanted to talk.'

'You were always…'

'No, you're forgetting, Ethel. We ate together. We walked almost every day. We sat together in the evenings, reading, listening to the radio. We went to church on Sundays. We played cards, remember? We went shopping. We worked in the garden. We went to concerts.'

'Scribbling. You were always scribbling,' her tone more hurtful than the kitchen knife.

The Colonel's story finishes. There's a peal of forced laughter. I wonder if he is a Colonel, if he's a guest or a patient, if Ethel has even talked to him.

'You didn't want me to join the VAD. You didn't want me to go.'

'I was anxious for you, that's all.'

The end of the yellow thread is sewn in, a bright orange one chosen.

'Remember that last concert we went to – the Philharmonic, in Aberdeen – Tannhauser?' I say. 'It wasn't so very long ago.'

> *Storm and sunshine on the seas*
> *amongst the furthest Hebrides.*

'Of course I remember.'

'There was a violinist with a beautiful face.'

> *M. To represent the human face. Add two dots for the*
> *eyes, thus ⁰M⁰. These dots, being equal to o's, we get omo*
> *(homo), Latin for man.*
>> *'Who reads the name*
>> *For Man upon his forehead, there the M*
>> *Had traced most plainly.'*
> *Dante: Purgatory xxiii*

I ease the pleats of my skirt into place.

'I've no idea what you're getting at… always hinting at something or other.'

'No, I'm not, Ethel… sorry, I just happened to remember.'

She studies where to insert the needle. 'Why didn't Walter come?'

'To the concert? Oh, sorry! Today? Did I not say? A meeting – an important one – of the Session: there's an ordination of Elders coming up.'

Me doh rae lah
Lah rae me doh.

She looks up from her work. 'You may as well go, then.'

'No dear, it's not time.'

She points the needle at me. 'That's half past two.'

No-one else in the room is moving. 'I've just arrived, Ethel. I'd to get two buses. It took me an hour and a half.'

'I didn't ask you to come.'

'But the doctor said… and I wanted to. I wanted to see you.'

She jerks her shoulder away.

Sometimes it only takes one more flake of snow to break the branch, but… not this time. So it's just in my mind that I stand up and walk to the door. I turn there, to look back. Even though I see her horrified expression – understand she's sorry that she's gone too far – I leave. She calls out after me, but something hard has crept up my spine. She'll never hurt me again. I keep walking along the corridors, out through the main door into air that's fresh and clear…

If it weren't for the letter from our bank manager in my handbag, I would have done it. But if I don't talk to her about it, I won't be able to reply. 'Well, look now. I'm very sorry, Ethel, but I have to ask you about something. I didn't mean to bring this up, not so soon, but we'll have to talk about it sometime, and it may as well be now. We need to decide what to do about the house.'

Her face says she isn't interested.

'We'll have to sell. That's the only option. It's what you want anyway… isn't it?'

She throws her embroidery away and jumps up. 'Don't you dare come near me!'

My hand flaps as if I'm trying to pat her back. I feel all the eyes in the room on us.

Her arms are waving so wildly she knocks her own glasses off. 'You take everything from me and it still isn't enough. It'll never be enough! Never!' I stand up to calm her but she shields her head as if expecting a blow.

'Don't, Ethel. Please don't.'

A nurse is coming over. I shake my head to let her know I didn't do anything, don't understand what's happening.

'Aw richt lass?' the nurse says.

'I told you she hates me.' Her body heaves with sobs.

My legs go from under me. I sit down again.

'There, there. Dinnae you fret.' The nurse puts an arm round Ethel's waist and steers her away.

'She didn't let Walter come.'

When my heartbeat's coming back to normal I pick up the specs and the embroidery, make sure the needle's safe, loosen the frame and straighten the fabric. The words Ethel is sewing are in verse.

Life out of death

Joy out of sorrow
The Cross today
The Crown tomo…

I hope there is a heaven, for her sake. And I hope papa's there to say he's sorry.

'*Ethel was mistaken. A misjudgement, that's all. Walter's explained everything to me and I'll explain it to her once she comes home… she's just been a little naïve. Bound to be upset, of course, but she'll get better, you know, with the help of the doctors, and our prayers. She'll understand, in time, why we'd to send her away.*'

Papa strides back and forward like that lemur the harbour-master's wife keeps in a cage. There are dark purple shadows under his eyes. He presses the fingers of both hands into his temple. 'I've a terrible headache.'

I say he should rest.

'*I must write to her,' he says. 'Before I do anything else. Have you written? Sent your love?*'

I want to grab him by the lapels. 'Papa, look at me!' I want to say. 'Will you just look at me? I know you've had a lot to worry about with Ethel, but why have you been avoiding me since I came back from Aunt Tweedie's? Have you not noticed anything? Do you not want to know what's wrong with me?'

I need to ask him how you can comfort someone else if there's a weight on your own chest that never goes away and your legs don't work properly and every step's an effort… you can't think straight, you don't know where to go, what to do, what to say.

I'll tell Ethel, if I write, she was lucky. At least she had a reason. The worst pain – worse than being betrayed – is not knowing why.

I want to shake papa. I know he's distracted – everyone is, for goodness sake. It's a tragedy for Ethel… but it isn't Walter's fault, goodness, no! He's been showing such promise in the ministry, and about to try for his own parish – well, maybe he'll leave that aside, for a few years, until things settle down. Amy'll be prepared to wait for her wedding. She can, can't she, now she's got what she wants?

And what a dilemma it is for papa, in his position, if the scandal gets out. I know he's worried about that. I wonder if it'd help if I tell him what he's been spared? It could've been so much worse.

His face seems to freeze for a second, then his pen dips into the inkwell. 'You should write to Ethel. She'd like that, a letter from you.'

Ethel didn't like my letter. Not at all.

Carved panels on the front of the doctor's desk. His hands are toying with the string of a binder – apart from a blotter and an inkwell, the only thing on the vast surface. 'Such a pity. Your sister's been doing so well.' One foot taps the floor. 'This seems quite out of character.'

It's always wise to smile. 'She seemed quiet, to begin with.'

'We pride ourselves – in this hospital… The prognosis for voluntary patients is usually very positive. Of course they're protected – we protect them – let's say from those more degraded in habit.' He pulls the string and takes some papers from the file. 'But, perhaps it was a blessing in disguise, this little incident. An insight. You understand?' He checks my agreement and attention over the top of his spectacles. 'Here, in trying to explain a person's predisposition to mental illness, we subscribe to the psycho-biological school of psychiatric medicine.'

'My brother-in-law recommended the hospital highly.'

He nods. 'His contribution to the board has been much appreciated. But... the business in hand. Now, what I want to say is, that the physical and psychological cannot be divorced.'

'I understand.'

'Psychosis – or neurosis – relieves tension in the individual.'

'Yes. I see.'

'A tension which comes from elsewhere. Well, that's the task, isn't it. To analyse the personality of the patient – your sister Ethel – and to consider what external factors may have affected her, or are affecting her.'

'Of course.'

'Our aim being to free her from suffering, to allow her to function normally.'

'That's what we all want.'

'So, for example, these recurring dreams of...' he's checking the notes – 'being burned alive. Now, you may know...'

I nod. It seems to be what he expects.

'You're in her dream. Perhaps you represent some aspect of the personality – the creative, perhaps? A poetess, you are, I believe? Of no small talent, so your brother-in law says, though your preoccupations... more of interest to the ladies, perhaps?'

My expression, I hope, is as inscrutable as my lips are tight.

'A striking image, don't you think, that her mind has conjured up – the Muse as bearer of fire – the force of ultimate destruction.'

From this floor there's an even better view of the grounds.

'Fascinating. Perhaps a fear of creativity itself – the chaos of creation?'

Clearing my throat is enough to convince him I agree.

'Of course, we mustn't forget the actual experience of the patient – past and present.' He draws himself up. 'Things she's done. What do you think, as her sister? What may have left a strong impression on her mind?'

I think he's about to tell me. 'Well, doctor. I'm not sure.'

'Come now. Just think about it. Fear and fire. Where have these two things come into conjunction with one another, and with Ethel?'

'Well... I suppose you mean her war service? But – that was more than ten years ago.'

'Some of us advised strongly against young women being sent to front-line field hospitals. Grotesque places, for those with delicate constitutions.' He leans back, folds his arms. 'And now we, as a society I mean, and they – of course – suffer the consequences. Her hospital came under heavy bombardment, didn't it? See what I mean?'

'Well, yes.'

'Her injury... not a gross disfigurement, of course, but perhaps enough to....'

'I see what you mean.'

'A subconscious memory, constantly triggered by a reminder – the facial scar? – might become an irrational fear.' He lets his pencil scan down the page, taps at a paragraph. 'So far so good.' His chair swivels so he can look out the window. 'But there's something else we'd like to get to the bottom of, and you're the very person to help. This idea that she's "wicked", in fact she has made the assertion – accusation?… possibly, but let's stick with assertion for the moment – that you, her sister, who might be expected to appreciate her qualities… if not to love her… in short, that you think she's "evil" and "hate" her. Now, may I ask? Can you cast any light on that?'

I spread my hands, palm up. 'I've never given her reason to believe that. On the contrary…'

He stops me with a hand held high. 'You won't mind, will you, if I just ponder aloud, for a moment?'

'Of course not.'

'Why, I ask myself? Why one particular person?'

'I haven't done anything…'

'No. Now please don't take this personally. No slur on your character, nothing like that. We're just trying to build up a picture, and from what we see, she's never been violent with anyone else.' His pen taps on the notes. 'You can confirm that?'

'As far as I'm aware.'

'And, eh' – he's like a conjurer building up to the climax of a trick – 'no-one else has even seen her "violence"? Heard the disturbance yes – your neighbours, I understand. But it's always when the two of you are alone.'

'We live together, doctor.'

He plays with his pen. The top joints of his fingers are long.

'She won't do anything, go anywhere, unless I'm with her.'

He underlines something in the file, flicks back a page, reads over a paragraph or two, looks up at last. 'Nothing then?' Tap, tap with the pen.

'Nothing.'

'When you and your brother-in-law brought her to the hospital she'd some quite serious contusions.'

I nod.

'Now that we've talked to her, you know, alone, when she was calm… if you could give me your version of events again, of what happened, that morning. If you don't mind? Perhaps you'll remind me? And please, remember, you're talking in confidence. You know, if you lost your temper or something… don't be afraid.'

I don't let him see I'm worried, just tell him what happened.

'You're absolutely sure that's the way it was?'

I'm very sure.

'And… well, is there anything you disapprove of, anything at all? In Ethel's manners, behaviour? Any animosity she may have picked up? '

'No.' His room seems colder than the rest of the hospital.

'Perhaps – subconsciously, of course – you might resent something?'

'Not at all.'

The bed is high. Papa lifts me up to see what mama has, some-

thing I'm going to like. I hold out my arms to mama. She's got a
bundle in a woollen shawl but enfolds me in her other arm. I get
to nuzzle into the new baby sister's neck.

He has a way of waiting.

'There was one thing... but it was so long ago.'

'Mm?'

'She... when she was a young woman.' My stomach ties itself
in a knot. 'She resented... took it very badly.'

'Badly?'

'Yes.'

He's waiting, so I've to go on.

'Father died. Of course, we all took it badly. But it was very
sudden, and Ethel was away at the time. In England. Mama
made me... wasn't able to, herself, she was distraught, as you
might imagine... she asked me to write.'

I say I can't do it.

Mama takes the handkerchief from her eyes and tells me it's
wicked to be wilful at such a time and God knows what she's
done to deserve this. It's my responsibility – nay, my duty – since
I've chosen not to take a husband when she's done all she can to
encourage me and now I'll have to buck up and stop pretending
I'm something I'm not, wandering on the hills writing poetry and
goodness knows what else I get up to... as if I don't have a home
to go to. Yes, I'll have to put my gallivanting days behind me now,
and dear God, it's just as well, isn't it...

None of us will have a home now because the presbytery will need the manse for the new minister. It's impossible to say yet how much money father's left although one thing's sure – it won't be enough to keep paying Ethel's fees at the hospital.

That's three daughters on her hands – she starts to sob again – only one of the three spoken for. If I'd only married well, as I could have done, she'd be looking forward to a comfortable old age instead of who knows what.

I stare at the blank paper. 'But how do I say it?'

She says, well that'll be a challenge won't it? Even people who fancy themselves as writers or poets sometimes have to come right out with something and just say it, straight, no nonsense, just as it is. 'Your father's dead. You'll have to come home.'

'But...'

'No.' she adds. 'Say... " as soon as we can make arrangements". We can't have her at the funeral.'

The altar and choir gallery were swathed in black: dignitaries, parishioners – people from all over the country were there. I didn't want them there. I didn't want black horses to pull the coffin. I didn't want people lining the streets. I didn't want the smell of hawthorn blossom, didn't want to see upturned grass and bare earth and baby George's grave dug up.

Ethel must have asked a nurse to post her reply. It arrived the day after the funeral.

I told Amy this would kill papa.

'Yorkshire, it was. She couldn't get back in time.'

He's interested.

I make light of it. 'Goodness, but that was thirty years ago!'

He looks grave. 'Interesting, though. Who knows the work-ings of the mind?'

Shutters come down over my eyes.

'All the philosophies, all the religions of the world – they accept death can be a great teacher. But which of us speaks with certainty? Ours may be a young science, yes, but it's a science, and we're learning all the time. Perhaps it'll be the honour of the psychiatrist to unlock the secrets.' He reaches for a book on the shelf beside him and rests his hands on the cover.

His satisfaction in touching a well-loved book almost makes me warm to him. I used to love the weight of Brewer's Diction-ary of Phrase and Fable, the smell and feel of the leather. I liked the shapes of sentences, quotations and paragraphs. I liked the sound and the rhythm of the words in my head. The letter M being special to me, I memorised what Mr Brewer had to say:

M this letter represents the wavy appearance of water and is called in Hebrew mem (water). Every word in the Materia More Magistralis begins with the letter M

Marion's misdemeanours mean my marauding militant monkey must minimise majestic mighty mountains. Maintaining magisterial momentum, mystic minstrels make melodious minuet music, mesmerising mild-mannered – mischievous – merry maidens.

'I must thank you for being frank. It's very important to be frank,' he's telling me.

I try to remember another attempt: I'm sure I had one that went on for a whole paragraph.

'Interesting!' He's writing a note in the file. 'I wonder... so!'

Another smile might be appropriate.

'Good. Let's move on.' He turns to the last page in the file. 'One last point then. A different aspect of the case. You recall the conditions of the voluntary patient?'

I'm not certain.

'As a voluntary patient Ethel can give us notice to quit. Three days – that's all that's generally required. And if she does that, well we'd feel inclined, you know, to let her go. That's really why I wanted to speak to you. Our willingness depends on the obligator's – that is your – willingness to receive the patient.'

'You think she's ready?'

'You don't want her home?'

'It's not that...'

'I must stress. Your sister gives us no trouble. Very industrious, very pleasant – biddable, helpful – with the nursing staff. Some slight confusion, worries – depression – hardly surprising, I'd say. And, if you think of her war experience, not unusual.'

'You make me a little hopeful.'

'I must tell you, she's quite a favourite with the nurses. Some of them had war service too, of course, one in the same hospital as your sister, though it was after her time.' His fingers slide down the pen. 'To be blunt, as far as we're concerned, Ethel could go home today.'

I'm surprised to see papa standing behind the doctor's shoulder, a lighted candle in his hand.

'But – you understand, stability is so very important. Now I'm not sure how you'll feel if – I should tell you we've talked to her about this. She'd prefer to stay with the Rev. and Mrs Nicol when she's released. But of course I wanted to check with you, to see what you'd think about that arrangement.'

'Stay with Amy?'

'A fresh start. It's what she wants – but of course you'd all have to agree.'

'My sister – Amy – doesn't keep too well.'

'Might even be a good thing – can't you see that? Make Ethel feel needed, give her a purpose. Perhaps you've tended to…'

It's a bleak, high moorland, and all the bonnier for that. A lisp o rain, the rocks glistenin wi damp. An outcrop o ancient rocks set in bracken, rounded hills and a wide valley: whaups on the skyline. A brown burn sings – croons. It flows through a clump of twisted junipers. A breeze rustles through the grasses; there's a taste o the sea on the wind.

I stretch out my arms.

Papa has gone. The doctor leans forward. 'Miss Angus? Are you all right?'

'Yes, thank you.'

'Well, I wanted to let you know what our thinking was. Perhaps you'll raise the matter with the Rev. and Mrs Nicol?'

'With the Rev. and Mrs Nicol?'

'We'd take it gradually, of course. We've a new rural retreat – a 'half-way' house – for the milder patients. We'd like to transfer her there – perhaps for a few days to begin with. Why don't you take her there this Sunday? We'll let them know to expect you. You can walk, sit in the garden, talk things over. The grounds are… some late flowering bulbs still out, I believe. And if Ethel likes it… well, we can be very flexible as to how we approach the next stage.'

'I'm not sure whether Rev and Mrs Nicol will be free on Sunday.'

'Do talk it over with them.'

CHAPTER 10

Greenock: May, 1930

There's not enough daylight to bring the stained glass window to life. That takes more than a wan imitation of the sun. But the radio forecast said it might brighten. If even one ray was to penetrate the clouds, and if I was looking at the right spot just when it hit – let's say passed through, these things pass through… a sunbeam would do.

Jesus wants me for a sunbeam.

If I was staring at the window, vigilant, it needn't even last: a twinkle would be enough. Eyes focussed on the halo of the saint, I settle back into the pew. My good ear is angled to the pulpit, to the timbre of Walter's voice. He's never really lost his accent. There's a vestige of the north-east in his vowels, if you know what to listen for.

'We ought, then, every one of us, approach with confidence…'

A natural pause in the sermon: the organist clears his throat, someone behind me sneezes. A tickle develops in my throat. If I start to cough I'll never stop. The woman beside me holds out an open bag of boilings, but I'm not sure I want one.

It sticks to my fingers, then – how it happens, I don't know – drops to the floor. At least that brings some colour to my cheeks. The noise tails off. The bag rustles again.

'No, thank you,' I signal.

'And if our ears were tuned to eternal harmonies'… Walter's an orator, like papa was, but fine words can't even begin to penetrate the gloom.

She's insisting.

'We should hear it in the voices of the day – and of the night; we should hear it in the sunshine and the storm; in the trees of the wood, as they rejoice before the Lord; in the waves of the sea, as they dash upon the shore; in the thunder as it rolls and mutters among the hills; in the cataracts as they fall.'

This is the only place I hear anything like poetry, these days.

> In the wild trumpet of the wind
> Beneath a moorland sky

> In the wind's wild trumpet
> across a moorland sky… across a moorland… across a
> blasted moor

Something like that: that's what I'd say. But I'm not sure even that would touch my soul. I sink back into a torpor with the rest of the congregation.

> *Ethel Mary, Ethel Mary…*
> *My age is sixteen,*
> *My father's a farmer on yonder green,*
> *He's plenty o money tae dress me sae braw,*
> *But there's nae bonnie laddie will tak me awa.*

'Three such beautiful daughters.' How courteous Walter seemed when papa first introduced him. But the way mama pushed us forward, and the way he looked each one of us up and down, in turn, I felt… humiliated. Mama had the best china out, on her best table-linen that was reserved for special occasions. She quizzed Walter – in the most polite manner, of course – about his family, his education, his hopes, his prospects. He acquitted himself admirably, if blandness is something you admire. That was probably the quality that endeared him to the elders of the parish kirk, who'd just appointed him. Personally, I'd hoped for more. Mama suggested Walter make a habit of dropping in, he should treat our home as a refuge until he found a satisfactory place of his own. We'd be delighted to see him. Nothing so vulgar as 'Wouldn't we, girls?' but we understood the requirement.

I excused myself for a previously arranged walking engagement with Margaret. Mama was none too pleased when I left, but by that time I was old enough… she knew better than argue. Margaret wasn't surprised to see me.

The sweet releases a sour centre that drags me back. Walter's patch of thin hair shows when he bows his head to pray. 'Strength and wisdom,' he beseeches, for us all, and – is he having trouble getting the word out? – 'patience'. Almost every head is bowed, just a few of us watch dust-motes in the air. I stretch my eyes into the distance.

> *M in numerals is the initial of mille, a thousand.*
> *'Whosoever prayeth for the soul of John Gower, he shall,*
> *so oft as he shall so doeth, have a M and a D days of*
> *pardon.' – Gower's Tablet.*

Beyond the great window, that's the real world. A person has to guard their eyes out there, in case someone sees into their soul. Here, in rows all facing the same way, we're safe – unless from the Almighty himself, but then he gave up on me long ago.

The edges of my Bible merge into its shadow. The leather cover is faded, smoothed where my fingers have rubbed. Its edges are worn, corners frayed, gilt lettering dulled. If I close one eye then the other – a trick from my childhood – it jumps from side to side.

Walter remembers the poor, and all those whose circumstances have been reduced – 'through no fault of their own'. And 'those who are sick' – a rustle from the petticoat of my neighbour, who was so sorry Mrs Nicol was missing another service – 'in body, and in mind'.

One of my thumbs scrapes at the cuticle of the other.

Mama's voice: 'A girl who doesn't know what to do with her hands is a pitiable object.'

Walter asks that we might – each and every one of us – be held in the warm light of God's love.

Any love.

Amen.

⁓

At lunchtime, Walter and Amy don't look at one another.

What was it Walter said about eternal harmonies? '... in trees rejoicing before the Lord, in waves dashing the shore' and somewhere else – but not in the manse.

I summon the effort to tell Walter it was a lovely service.

'Thank you, Marion.'

I compliment Amy on the quality of the lamb in the stew.

She nods, curtly.

All adore Amy.

Ambitious and ambiguous as an anxious angel.

It's hard to keep it up, but harder to sit in silence. 'Amy,' I say, 'I know you're worried. But please don't worry. I'll do anything I can to help.'

She pushes cabbage around her plate, letting her knife scraik against the china.

'What I thought was, if I've to sell the house, and – obviously

– I don't see a way round that, I could find accommodation…
nearby, I mean. Near here. Then Ethel can have your guest
room, and I'll be on hand to help.'

A look passes between them.

Walter tells me not to even think about renting a room,
they've discussed this and if I do have to sell my little house –
but of course it may not come to that, there's always a chance
things will improve – there will always be a bed for me in
the manse, whatever happens regarding Ethel. There are two
perfectly decent rooms in the attic that they would've furnished
already, if they'd been required, but of course with just the
two of them there was no need. Ethel and I could both move
in there – with our own furniture – and they'd be on hand to
help if any problems arose, though hopefully the hospital will
have sorted everything out. He recognises, they recognise, that
eventually, if Ethel settles properly, I may want to move on.
They'd quite understand.

'Be just like the old days.' Amy doesn't try to pretend she'd
anything to do with Walter's plan. 'Living together again, the
three of us. Ridiculous. My God!'

'I agree with Amy, Walter. It wouldn't work. Better if I move
out right away.'

The lines on Amy's face drag downwards. If she was a dog
she'd be a bulldog, snarling. "But you're the oldest. You're the
one…' My body's pinned to the back of the chair. 'Mama told
you to take care of Ethel. What am I supposed to do? After all
those years? I hardly know her.'

'Look, it might not come to anything. I know what she's like.

And there are steps to be gone through. Absolutely nothing's certain yet.'

She pays no heed.

'I'm telling you, Walter. I can't do it. Won't.'

I steady myself with my hands flat on the table. 'Don't think for a minute any of this was my idea. If I'd any choice in the matter...'

'And we've really no choice, Amy. If that's what the doctors recommend, well, we must accept they're the ones who know best.' Walter's voice has taken on an edge.

'That's what you'd like to think.' Her knife and fork slam down.

'You have to be aware it's a very delicate position for me.'

'They don't know the half of it, do they? The doctors.'

'They've Ethel's best interests at heart.'

'What if we tell them?'

'Tell them?'

'What it's all about.'

'We don't know "what it's all about" Amy, as you put it. They wouldn't be interested in that.'

'You can't make me have her here.'

His pulpit voice: 'Amy, it's the very least we can do in the circumstances – she's your sister, after all. You must take it seriously. You've a certain responsibility.'

'How dare you! I haven't done anything wrong. I didn't. Do. Anything. Wrong.' She's rapping the table with a knuckle, each one more emphatic than the last. 'It was your fault. And all these bloody years this has festered. I'm sick of it.'

I float near the ceiling, looking down on them as if they're strangers. Last night I dreamed I was starting to die. I was tempted to let it happen, but something – can't remember what – made me come back.

'There's no advantage in bringing that up now Amy, and certainly no benefit in using bad language.'

'Ethel's cunning. You don't realise.'

'She's unhappy, that's all,' he coaxes. 'We can all be mature about this, can't we? Surely we can provide her with some little comfort until she's on her feet again.'

'I don't trust her.'

'And what if we turn her away? What'll people say?'

'I'm past caring.'

'It's not just my reputation I'm talking about, dear. I've to think of the church.'

Amy shudders. I concentrate on the hallmark of my fork.

Walter adjusts his cuff-links. 'Look, things'll work out. What if we were to introduce her to… what if she were to get involved in the Fellowship? It'd save you so much work. You don't really enjoy that side of things, do you, dear? And it might just be the making of her. Remember how good she was at organising bazaars?'

Amy's head rests on her hands. Mama wouldn't approve of elbows on the table. I refrain from saying so.

Walter looks from Amy to me, and remembers I'm here. 'Marion's already shouldered more than a fair share. Yes, it could work out. Marion, don't you think so?'

The wound on my finger is still quite raised and red: the edges are taking their time to knit together. There are liver spots and blue veins on the backs of my hands.

'Let's all go into it together, one step at a time – it shouldn't be beyond us! Not with God's help.'

I almost feel sorry for him.

'And this afternoon… we take our first tentative step.'

Amy's playing with a griggle on the tablecloth.

'Well, you know, my mind's made up. I'm going. This very afternoon. I'm driving Ethel out into the countryside. And you're coming too, Amy. We're just taking her for a little run in the car. What could be more normal than that? And we've to be home in time for the evening service, so it'll be a quick trip.'

He checks with me.

I nod rather than say anything that would side with him against Amy.

'Marion's coming too. See? Despite everything, she hasn't given up.'

'Marion's different from me. Always has been.'

I almost knock my chair over as I shove it back. 'Oh, I know, I know. Don't worry, I'm well aware, dear of what you think. You don't like my opinions, what I wear, the way I cut my hair. You never have. You don't approve of my friends, my habits, my "poetry". I'm not "normal"… whatever that is.' I clutch the back of my chair so hard one of my fingers cramps.

'Rather overwrought, aren't you?'

'A "normal" reaction, I'd say. "If you prick me, do I not bleed?"'

'What d'you say?'

'Nothing.'

'I hate it when you do that. I suppose it's from one of your poems, is it?'

'Yes,' I say.

'Come, come!' Walter tells her I'm teasing. 'It's from a play, actually, dear. Merchant of Venice. Shakespeare. You must have read it at school.' He rises. 'I want you to come this afternoon, Amy. You owe it to Marion – and to me.'

'And to Ethel?'

'You know I'm right.'

'You know I'm not well.'

He swallows hard.

I walk to the window, but there's nothing worth looking at. Everything's smothered in dirt, even the last clump of bluebells by the side of the path. 'Amy, do you ever worry you might be... a little bit unsound? Sometimes I do. I wonder – about myself, I mean. If it's a family thing...'

She doesn't answer.

Walter studies his pocket-watch. 'I make very few demands on you, Amy.' His voice is quiet. 'But on this occasion I'm going to insist you come with me. I'm going to get the car ready now, and will be back in ten minutes.' As if nothing untoward has happened, he turns at the door and reminds Amy that the fresh air will do her so much good.

'Well, won't this be cosy.'

I answer despite my better judgement. 'He's trying his best.'

'What would you know?'

'Well, you're right there, of course. What would I know, an old spinster like me? But let me tell you something.' I need to say my piece. Say it now. Maybe this isn't the best time, but it'll do till a better one comes along. 'You should never assume anything... about anyone.' My voice has found an old strength.

'I don't know what you mean.'

'No, you wouldn't.'

'Well, I don't need to assume much about you, do I? My God! D'you think people don't notice the sly little hints, the innuendo... D'you understand how they laugh, behind your back? To write the way you do... a spinster, not just a spinster, but at your age... how can you? "Faeries" are bad enough, but you should have stuck to them. Lovers! You're deranged. How d'you think mama would have felt? How d'you think I feel?' She scrapes the plates and clatters the dishes as she stacks them. 'You're a laughing stock.' Her face is more animated than I've seen it for a long time.

'Well, at least that's out in the open. Now let me finish.'

She pointedly stops clearing the table.

My courage is draining fast. 'You seem to think love is, you know, something you hoard. Well, it isn't. It isn't like a purse full of money you save up then dole out for whatever you want. "Here, this is for you; here you are, take this; here my darling sister"' – she doesn't like sarcasm – '"this is for you – oh, sorry, I'll have to take it back, I've hardly any left!"'.

'Rather clichéd, don't you think?'

'I thought you might understand a cliché.' It isn't anger that's making me shake, it's rage, pure rage. I wonder where it's come from. 'You of all people should know that you don't – you can't – nobody controls love.'

'That's your message? Is that it? Your legacy to the world? Is that what your poems are all about?'

'Love finds you, whether you're looking for it or not. When and where you least expect it. And when it does you should take heed, because… because your capacity to love grows stronger, the more you embrace it.'

Her napkin's folded and rolled and pushed into its ring.

'And you grow stronger.'

'You don't know what you're talking about.'

'No? And maybe you don't either. Whatever it is you feel seems to have brought you nothing but bitterness. I'd hate to be bitter.'

'I just wish I knew what you did to make it all flare up again.'

'Pardon?'

'Anyway, it's all your fault.'

'Meaning?'

'I should've known better than listen to you. You and that old gypsy Nellie whatever-her-name-was.'

'What does Nellie have to do with anything?'

'Her stupid ideas. I knew it was wrong. Just tried it out of curiosity.'

'Tried what?'

'That arm-pit thing.'

∽

'They try to be kind. Some of them are very kind.' Ethel's prim and tidy. Though the red lips take a bit of getting used to, the hairstyle's a definite improvement. She's on her best behaviour: excited, but holding herself back – quite properly. There's nothing in her demeanour to say there's anything wrong.

But the conversation with the psychiatrist replays in my head, makes it difficult not to be apprehensive. All I can do is try, and hope.

'Of course, it's not entirely suitable for me.' Amy's awkward hug is endured.

Walter's hands enclose her two. 'Just a short-term measure, dear. Expedient. Until you're sufficiently rested.'

'I'm not going to dwell on it, not today.'

She runs her fingers along the curves of the car bonnet, studies the RAC badge. 'I can't tell you what this means to me! It's such a beautiful car, Walter. And such a shine on it… '

'I gave it a clean it before we came out.'

'You cleaned it for me!'

He bends the truth a fraction, in the tone and the omission. Yes, well, he does rather take a pride in it. Keeps it polished as a precaution against the salt air that's so very corrosive – doesn't want spots of rust.

'You're so meticulous, Walter. I always appreciated how meticulous you were.' She lets that sink in.

I tell myself it's a perfectly normal conversation.

'And "Morris",' she's saying, 'That's the manufacturer. Not the name of the car!'

We make a show of appreciating the joke.

'You see, I'm not entirely ignorant!'

It's on the tip of my tongue, but Amy gets in first. 'Should we make a start?' She opens the front passenger door.

Ethel stands in her way. 'May I?' she says. Amy looks at Walter. 'No, no, I don't mean for the journey, Amy. Just to try it, the front seat.'

'You don't mind, dearest?'

Amy knows better than admit it.

'Thank you so much.'

Amy keeps hold of the door so Ethel can't close it. Ethel settles herself back, asks Walter about this dial and that dial on the dashboard, this switch and that. He explains everything in detail.

'Such a long time since I've been in a car!'

'Walter brought you and Marion all the way from Aberdeen in this very car.'

A sharp response: 'I was in a state of nervous debility that day, Amy, as you well know. Not myself at all.' But she recovers quickly. 'I'm so looking forward to this afternoon. You'll see. It's going to be lovely.'

Walter puts an arm round Amy. 'My dear, why don't we let Ethel travel in front? She'll get a better view of the countryside.'

'No, no, I just wanted to try it, see what it was like. I sometimes used to sit in the front of the ambulance, you know. We took turns to go out.' She picks up her handbag, pretends to look for something in it. We wait. 'Well, just if you really didn't mind, Amy?'

Walter steers Amy towards the back. 'It isn't too much to ask, dear. Just for this once.'

Amy climbs in the back. I walk round to the other side. Walter holds the door open for me too. 'For pity's sake, Walter, let's go.' I say. 'Let's just get there, get it over with.'

Everything looks fresher when we leave the city behind. The sky opens up, there's a green blush on the fields. The blossom's out by the roadside. I admire, aloud, a bank of beautiful rhosidandrums.

Amy wonders why I persist in using such silly old-fashioned words.

The river traffic's quiet, it being a Sunday, but one merchant ship, pilot alongside, is sailing downriver. Ethel's looking out the window, enjoying the drive, I tell myself. Walter points out Dumbarton Rock, tells us something about a letter from St Patrick.

My attention's been taken by a track that follows the bank of the river. It disappears now and then, behind trees, cottages, an occasional warehouse, but always re-appears. I wonder how far it goes.

The river gets wider, the valley broader. I can't see the path now, but there's a hedgerow, and I deduce it must be behind that. I want it to be there.

Walter turns away from the river at a junction. 'Just two miles from here, the doctor said.'

We're on a single-track road, lots of bends and hedges that hide what might come round the next corner. I miss the open views of the river. I miss the path. The motion of the car is beginning to make me nauseous.

Amy says we've just passed the entrance.

Walter drives another mile before he's able to turn. He drives back slowly and finds the gate.

Amy's half-turned away from me, looking out the window.

'Almost there, sweetheart,' I hear from the front. I glance at Amy but don't think she heard.

Walter's concentrating on his driving, as the track is quite narrow. The tyres crunch on the gravel. Ethel's hand is resting on Walter's arm.

I lean forward and grip her shoulder. 'This looks like a grand place to recuperate, Ethel.'

Her eyes sparkle. There are two pink spots on her cheeks. She covers her mouth loosely with one hand. 'It'd be such a lovely place for a wedding!'

Walter parks and shuts the engine off, gets out of the car to stretch his legs then – gentleman that he is – goes to open Ethel's door.

Amy's slumped in her seat.

Someone's been watching for us because the front door of the house opens. A lady waves across. Walter acknowledges her. Ethel clutches his arm and pulls him away from the car.

'You coming, Amy?' I say.

The hem of her coat catches in the car door. 'That bitch is up to something.'

'Come on. We'll split them up.'

'I knew no good would come of this.'

Walter and Ethel shake hands with the lady in the porch. They look round as Amy and I arrive at the door.

'And this is my sister,' Ethel says. 'She's been so looking forward to coming.'

Walter looks confused.

I push myself forward. 'How do you do. I believe you're expecting us?'

'And are you all richt, dearie?'

'Thank you. A little nausea in the car.'

'Of course.'

'Would it be all right if… I'd like to walk round the garden before we come in. If that's all right?'

There's no problem, she understands I'm a little anxious – we all look a little anxious. She'd have suggested it herself.

'Thank you so much,' I link an arm into Ethel's and gesture with Walter to do the same with her other arm. We find the strength to make her walk with us.

'Can I help?' the lady says. 'Would you like some help?'

'It's just that she needs a little air,' Ethel calls back. 'We won't be long.'

'Follow the path, then. You can't go wrong. It'll take you all the way round the estate. Half an hour, at the most. And have a wee look in the walled gairden – it's very restful. Then we'll have tea, and talk things through and I'll show you the accommodation.'

'Ethel, you're confused,' I say, when we're out of earshot.

'You are.'

'This is part of the hospital. The doctors thought you could recuperate here.'

'If only you knew how tiresome she can be!' she says to Walter.

'Stop it Ethel!'

'"She'll make trouble," I told you that, didn't I?' She stops so suddenly that I almost fall over. 'No. That was Amy, wasn't it.'

'Ethel!'

'Hush, Marion. Stop interfering.'

I hope Amy stays where she is, talking to the lady. 'Please, let's have a nice afternoon, Ethel. A little walk, a cup of tea, then perhaps a chat.'

Flies buzz round our heads. Trying to brush them away, Ethel pulls away from us. 'Don't touch me!'

Walter plants himself in front of her and grips the tops of her arms: 'Ethel, please. We all care for you. We want the best for you. Marion, and Amy and I...'

'Amy?' She calls back over her shoulder. 'Oh, Amy! Thank you so much! You want the best for me. The best man? Thank you! Thank you! And for you... is it a baby, you want now? Is that what it is? The best baby? A girl, is it? A dear little thing?'

Luckily Amy's in the house now. But Walter doesn't know where to look.

'Don't worry, Walter my love. We'll let her stay, ' Ethel says. 'We won't put her out.'

'Tell her, Walter, for God's sake, tell her.'

It wasn't papa's place to do it. It should have come from Walter. And he must say it now, straight, the way it was, the way it is.

I don't love you. Never loved you.

Ethel waits: not a shred of doubt on her face.

Walter looks at her, touches her cheek. He wants nothing more than to take her pain away... of course he loves her, doesn't he love all of God's creatures, even the sick and the lame. If only she'd…

'You're such a bloody coward, Walter,' I say.

'Coward?'

'You need to stop this, once and for all.'

'Be quiet, Marion. Everything's going to work out,' Ethel says.

Walter grasps at her words. 'What do you mean, Ethel, "work out"?'

'I'm going to lift the curse,' she says.

'Pardon?'

'I can do that. Some people can. If you try hard enough. You know, make things happen – or not.'

Walter might be about to collapse.

She points at me. 'Ask her. She knows.'

I shake my head.

'It's not the way you think. Not broomsticks and cauldrons, not that kind of thing. Cats! No, not cats. I don't like cats. Just – a kind of prayer. The same as papa used to say – "if you pray hard enough…" and are patient. I've been very patient, haven't I?'

Nellie fills her pipe and tells me a tale.

A wee lass, it was, watchin fower ploughs workin a field. 'I could stop all thae ploughs,' she says tae her faither.

'Show me,' he says, thinkin it bairn's talk.

She says some words. Three o the ploughs stop. 'The ither ploughman must hae a sprig o rowan on the halter,' she tells her faither, 'tae keep the horsie safe.'

The man grabbed his wee lass and shook her. 'Wha showed ye how tae dae that?'

'My nurse.'

The dochter was bled tae death by a surgeon. Her auld nurse was burned on a blackthorn pyre.

Ethel sidles up to Walter. She leans her head against his chest. Her arms go round his neck.

I'd strangle him, if I were her.

'Anyway, it was all Marion's fault, in the very beginning – if it hadn't been for her none of the bad things would've happened. Papa wouldn't have got so upset. He sent her away, you know.'

My limbs are heavy.

'Ethel, it was you who went away. To the hospital.'

'He sent you away first.'

A voice like that never lies.

'Stop! Both of you,' Walter says.

Papa sent me away first, to Aunt Tweedie. She's right. Everything slows down. Lines etch themselves on my forehead.

Walter's pulpit voice is droning on.

I back away, so I won't see the pieces of the jigsaw falling into place.

It's nae whaur ye've been, it's whaur ye gae next, that matters.

The overgrown track pulls at my feet. It's going to take me to the river. When I come to the shore, I'll turn west and keep walking – I know there's a path, I've seen it. – it'll take me to the coast, then north, eventually. I've never been to these hills on the west, not to where the Atlantic Ocean batters the foot of great cliffs and stacks of bare rock scratch at the sky. I can do it. I can go there, if I just keep walking.

I'll get my rhythm back, with luck and the wind behind me. I check inside my bag. Yes, it's there, my notebook.

PART III

CHAPTER 11

Banchory: May, 1945

A bracken-covered hill at sunset, the ruins of a sheepfold. I count foxgloves, pause at the cry of a peewit.

A wheel squeaks: cups rattle on a trolley. Someone pokes my shoulder. Jolted awake, I'm muddled. My eyes search for light, settle on wee rectangles: the blinds are pulled well down to keep out the late spring chill. My hands need a rub, to get the circulation going, but that's too much effort. I remember: the fire's lit at tea-time, not a second before. Still, be grateful, made it through another winter – and another war. That must be an achievement of a kind. Things are bound to improve.

'Telephone message for you.'

The woman's voice always sets my nerves on edge.

'A Miss Greig. Coming to see you.'

Half of my newspaper lies crumpled at my feet.

'Who?'

'Miss Williamina Greig.'

I grope under the chair cushion. My knuckle scrapes the wooden frame of the chair. I'd cradle the sore bit for a second, but don't want her to notice.

'She said you'd remember her as Minnie.'

The pencil is stuck in the crease between the arm and the seat. I can't get a grip. 'Minnie?'

She's puts a match to the fire then stands before me with her arms folded. From the smell, the tea's stewed, and that's a blessing.

'I was Minnie, once.'

'Miss Williamina – Minnie – Greig. Pleasant sounding lady, very polite.' She makes sure her words are loud enough for everyone to hear. 'From Arbroath.'

'A long time since I was there.'

'Used to be housekeeper to your late friends, I believe. Mr and Mrs Cunningham.'

I feel the heat already, and begin to feel more human.

'Miss Greig hasn't seen you for a long time.' She draws in her cheeks. 'You didn't manage to go to the funeral.' The tone of her voice is thinner. Some of the other residents perk up. A relief of tedium always welcomed.

I guess the number of patterns across a curtain and count the number of rows in the length, multiply by two for each window then by four for all the windows in the room. Suddenly it comes to me.

'Real fun. Funeral.' I can't believe I was foxed: such a simple anagram.

It takes her aback for a moment but she recovers. 'Have you no respect?'

'No, I mean, it's a clue. The crossword, you know… in today's P & J.' I can't reach the pages on the floor but the headlines are so big and bold I could read them from this distance even if I didn't remember what they said. And I want to believe it, but when you've believed it all before… who can say? Maybe the world will be a better place, but all I know is the end of a war can be a time of reckoning. For everybody.

She scoops up the newspaper with one hand, pinches my arm with the other. I never understand how she thinks she can hurt me like that.

Something like vigour in her voice: 'I took the liberty of telling Miss Greig you'd be at home on Friday.' She beams around the room, straightens the pages of my paper, lays it beyond my reach.

I don't want her to see me with a blanket across my knees. The skirt and blouse I keep for when the minister comes is still decent, and I'm wearing the pearls. Little more than a smell in my compact – a few grains of powder round the rim, but I dabbed the puff on my cheeks anyway.

She'll be bringin me a 'minding' from Margaret's jewel box, and it'd be churlish to say I've no need of a brooch. The lassie could've posted it and saved the train fare so the least I can do is thank her very much, ask about Robert and Margaret, for auld time's sake. What it was like for them, the war, and how Robert coped with his illness. But did he seem content in himself? Then I'll wonder how she's doing herself, Miss Minnie Greig, and now they've gone and the war being over and where is she staying? She surely never took a husband then? But she's still at an age to enjoy the grand new world that'll come, surely, once we get over the shortages.

And aye, if she asks I'll tell her how lucky I am being here, so near the hills, everything I need at my fingertips and the food – many's the one fared far worse through the war – and the staff pleasant enough, though you always get the odd one...

Then that'll be that. She'll go away and for a while, when I'm trying to sleep, a warm trickle on my cheek might surprise me, but the memory will fade – memories always fade – back there into the shadows.

My fingers are locked together, my thumbs white with the pressure. I ease them apart and brush an invisible crumb from my lap.

Miss Williamina Greig.

A warm, firm shake, and she doesn't want to let go my hand. A smile that's trying to break through, though she doesn't like to assume... hesitant, just like a candle flickers before the wick catches properly, in the way she says hello.

The family likeness is more marked than I remember. She's thinner, that's why. What am I thinking about? We're all thinner.

She's squatting at my feet.

My hand reaches out to touch the silver in her hair. It used to be black, blue-black. She twisted it in a bun with one hand: an old style for a young lass, I always thought, even one with a wise head on her shoulders.

'Ye do mind me?' She pulls grit from the corner of her eye. 'At Mr and Mrs Cunningham's? Ye do!' Her face does everything it can to encourage me.

I want to speak.

She stands up and looks round, taking her time. Most of the other residents are dozing, a few reading. As she turns back, she rests her hand on my shoulder – a wee touch, hardly there at all, but enough. 'You're teasing': the words surer than the tone.

A nervous laugh is all I manage.

The lines at the side of her eyes crinkle up. 'You do so mind!'

Walking the hills, sitting by the loch-side, warming ourselves when we got in, by the kitchen stove, talking into the night, reading together... laughing. I put a hand to the place where the words get stuck. You sometimes have to rub, a little bit, even if it hurts, to get them moving.

'Fine you do.'

Listening to the wireless, choosing which record to play... her gramophone was her pride and joy. It isn't what I want to say but it's a start: 'Miss Greig, my memory may no longer be what it was but I can understand mair than ae phrase at a time.'

She hugs me. 'Listen tae you! That's mair like it!'

Her smell's clean and sharp.

'My God, if ye just kent... I've been like a hen on a het griddle.'

My face is still pressed against her coat. Vinegar, that's what the smell is... the nap of her collar's been refreshed with vinegar. She feels me loosen up, lets go and steps back.

'What is it?'

'Just… your turn o phrase. It's good tae hear you again.'
Vinegar. Isn't that… that mindfulness, isn't that just like her?

*A brass angel it was, the doorbell. Wires ran up the wall and
through hoops, and while I'm trying to work out what to pull or
push the door opens. I jump back. The beam on her face fades. She
gives a hint of a curtsey then covers her mouth and says she's sorry
she didnae meant tae fleg me, she could kick hersel, she should hae
waited for the bell but she heard me arrive and the butterflies in
her belly…*

*I say 'How do you do?' and she says Mr and Mrs Cunningham
are very, very, very sorry but they were summoned this very
afternoon tae the notary in Blairgowrie for a bit o business, and
there was nothin they could dae but go. She bobs up and down
again. She's tae look after me and she's sorry, she kens she's nae
very guid at curtseys yet – she's just been wi Mrs Cunningham
for three months and twa weeks and fower days, and maist things
she's a quick learner, but her knees get in the road o a curtsey. Mrs
Cunningham says it's maybe auld fashioned but times it's res-
pectful, and this is maybe ane o thae times, for she wants tae mak
a guid impression.*

I ask if she'd let me come in then.

*Dearie me! She's that sorry for keeping me on the doorstep, how
is it when ye try the hardest ye mak the maist mistaks?*

*I'm ushered inside, my bag carried for me. The house is grand:
everything solid and smooth and polished. I admire the panelling,
the line of the stair, the curves of the balustrade. Light floods into*

the hall through the stair window. My hand rests on a Chinese vase.

'Ane o a pair.' *The other's in an alcove on the opposite side.* 'Mr Cunningham brocht them back frae his travels.'

'Yes, Miss...' *It's been a while, but I slip back into it naturally:* 'You hae the advantage, Miss...'

'Oh, for the love o... backside foremaist again!' *She holds out her hand.* 'Miss Williamina Greig – that's my Sunday name, I'm 'Minnie' tae everybody – housemaid tae Mr and Mrs Robert Cunningham. Pleased tae be o service tae you, madam.' *She makes another stab at a curtsey, but she's playin it up this time.*

'I was called Minnie, when I was wee,' *I tell her.*

She's made rock buns. We eat in the kitchen, at my request, and afterwards she takes me to the turret room.

My fingers trace the leaded panes as I take in the view up the glen; the lower slopes of the hills; a glimpse of reed beds, of the lochan, of a fairy knoll on the other side of the river.

She checks the surface of a table. 'I gied it a richt guid dust for ye.'

Below, the garden: a shrubbery and herbaceous border, a path leading into a clump of silver birch. 'Mrs Cunningham kent you'd like it here.'

'Aye,' *I say,* 'She kens me well. She was right. I like it.'

If I pull the table across to the window, nobody can come into the house without me seeing. If I keep the door ajar, nobody can climb the stairs without me hearing.

'I mind the door-bell,' I say and tell her that if she's bidin a wee while, she should take her coat off.

'We need some licht in here.' Without as much as a 'by your leave' the blinds are raised and the curtains pulled back as far as they'll go.

The light shows up the faded chairs, but it's a grand room.

'There.' She settles herself in a chair and takes my hand in hers. 'I hoped, ye ken, but I wouldnae hae been surprised if you'd forgotten. You being a famous poet, me just a housemaid.'

'Ye're still a bit o a blether!' The words and the sound the-gither... somethin's there, in my voice. I hardly dare think it's mine.

'Well, I thocht ye were famous.'

'That's a different thing.'

'You were on the wireless. I didnae ken naebody else that had been on the wireless.'

'Well, I've given that all up. Poetry, I mean.'

'Aye, I'll believe that.'

'No, I have. Plain speakin's better, if you've somethin to say.'

A good-natured shove: 'Awa!'

'That's what my mama always said.'

'That maks it true?'

'Miss Greig... Minnie, it must be, what? Fifteen years?

'Sixteen, since we last met. And d'ye mind... when we first went up the hill? Mr and Mrs Cunningham awa for the day – you helped me wi the chores, then we climbed tae the lochan?'

'I mind.'

'You pointed tae a cave on the cliff and said that was whaur the last wolf in Scotland had its lair. And me, I'd never been higher than the Law in Dundee... God, but did I sweat! You near twice my age, and never tired. But I was that determined tae keep up. I huffed and puffed and never let on, just kept gaein.'

'That's what you've to do, sometimes.'

'Then ye went for a swim. Mind that? You took yer claes aff, bold as brass and waded richt in. "The water's fine", ye said and the fleg I got, it was that cauld! You tried tae mak me float.'

'I mind holdin the back o your head.'

'And you swam richt across.'

'It's a gey wee lochan.'

'Ye made it look easy.'

Neither of us ken what to say next. I break the silence. 'I've never thocht aboot that cave for years.'

She sits back. 'The pity was you didnae come mair often.'

'Miss Greig – Minnie – these were difficult times. But what I've aye remembered, what I mind best, is that you were very, very generous.'

Never could hide what she was thinkin.

'Wi your time. And your friendship.'

'It went the baith weys.'

'Things were very hard, for me, for a while.'

'I ken that.' Her gaze straight and strong and there's a hint o reproach. 'Just... I'd hae liked ye tae keep in touch. Letters, if that was all.'

'Gettin through each day was a struggle.'

'You didnae answer my letters.'

'Please don't, dinnae think... I didn't... I moved about such a lot. I didn't even get all my letters. And... she needed you, didn't

she, Robert being away so much? She wouldn't have liked it…
whatever we thought at the time.'

'I thocht maybe that cam intae it.'

She clears her throat. 'Well – if ye dinnae mind me sayin it –
ye were far too saft, Mrs Cunningham thocht, for your ain guid.
Aye takin on ither folk's problems. She said it was very sad, you
cuttin yersel aff, the wey ye did, frae yer friends, the very folk
that had loved ye since ye were a lassie.'

'Margaret said that?'

'Och, often she'd a wee worry aboot you. Him tae, but he aye
said "We've to respect her wishes, Margaret. She kens fine our
door's aye open."'

'I didn't like to impose.'

'She aye put on a good show – had that much tae say for hersel
didn't she? But there was times she was gey low.'

'She must hae missed him, when he was gone.'

'She'd got used enough tae it, when he was traipsin the world.'

'Did he ever settle?'

'Thae last ten years, mair or less.'

'I did write, when I heard he was ill, and again when he died.'

'She said.'

'I didnae think I'd anything to offer.'

'Friendship would hae been enough.'

She's lifting my other hand and sees me wince. The blood
drains from my face. 'What is it?' I try to take my arm away but
there's no strength in it. The cuff of my cardigan is lifted back.
'How'd ye get that?'

'Och, it's just my age. I mark easily. At the slightest thing.' I pull the sleeve back down. 'I didnae mean to hurt Margaret, you ken. I just… I didnae want to be a burden.'

'Now you listen. I didnae mean ye tae tak offence. Of course ye didnae.' She looks at her watch. Her fingers tap a rhythm on the chair. 'Listen, I should… I want tae tell ye how I'm here. It's maybe daft, turnin up like this. I could've written, when I found oot whaur ye were, but, ach, I thocht, "she'll just ignore a letter." '

'Aye?'

'Mrs Cunningham, afore she died, she tellt me tae think aboot it.'

'About?'

'Look, I dinnae ken whaur I get my brass neck, but Mrs Cunningham said, what wi you and my mither bein the best o pals and she kent how much I liked you – and your poems – and thae bein sic terrible times, what was the point in haudin back? I'd nae family tae speak o and you'd nae family left and the twa o us would get on that well thegither.'

'Margaret always liked to…'

'Aye, organise folk.' She leans forward. 'But she meant well – a hert o gold. Well, listen, this is it. I'm nae sure how ye're placed, but, ach, I've a plan micht just suit the baith o us.' She pauses for breath.

I don't say anything.

'Maybe this time it'll work oot.'

CHAPTER 12

∽

Banchory: June, 1945

Private hotels are all so much of a muchness. If anyone should know that, it's me. This one was far enough away from anyone – but it was the setting that really made the difference. Just knowing they were out there, on the doorstep, the hills, the moors, and through the passes, beyond, the glens of Angus.

I went back to Glen Dye, one last time: took the bus from Banchory. From the Cairn o Mount road the landscape looked bleak – and God, it was bonnie. My legs were slow, but I stopped and rested beside the water – was tempted for a moment, no more than that, by yon still pool. But Clach-na-ben beckoned and I thought, just one more time. I summoned everything to keep going, made it to the top, hoisted myself up the tor, foothold by foothold, inch by inch to the very spot where the witch is buried, where I found the little rock ledge strewn with feathers and bones, where Wull would wait, his back against the rock – him coming up from Deeside, watching the horizon, as

I crossed from Glen Esk.

From the tor, the Water o Dye was nothing but a line, like something drawn on a map, and the pool a black dot, nothing of consequence. My eyes swept the slopes to the sea. From this distance it looked still, but I knew well the tide would be dragging at the shingle, waves would be crashing against rocks, the wind would be blowing salt spray over somebody's hard won fields.

Lightsome on my feet, I stretch my arms out. My body's in perfect balance. The wind tugs at my sleeves…

I close my eyes for a second. No, no. I didn't try to fly, not that last time. I wasn't even bold enough to get off the bus – hard enough getting on, the step so high. But people were kind. A wee girl moved out of the front seat for me and when I changed my mind and told the conductor I'd just go on to Fettercairn he said thank goodness, he was worried sick at the thocht o leavin me at the back o beyond. He didn't even charge the extra fare.

Nearly everyone's finished eating, but I haven't started my soup. If I don't speak now it'll be too late. I can do it. I can. But it's so long since I'd anything to say. It's not like a quiet mutter you have with the person in the next chair, or the head-down apology that you're bothering somebody with something trivial. You've to expand the lungs. I summon an image of papa – don't often think of him now – the way he stood in the pulpit, shoulders back, hands on the brass rail. Two breaths, then two more.

I might even miss some of these people, I realise, but that's a risk worth taking. 'There's something I want to tell you.'

Conversations stutter to a halt. The words, unexpectedly exposed, leave a trace like a curl of smoke from a fire. Folk lean forward to make sure it was me that spoke.

'I'm going home.'

Sideways glances between neighbours.

'To Arbroath. At the end of the week.'

Disbelief – furrowed brows.

'I've engaged a maid – a kindly lady.'

Everyone talks at once.

'But you like it here, well enough, don't you?'

'You've been here for so long!'

'None of us are as fit...' she looks round for confirmation and support. 'With your health, Miss Angus?'

'And whaur will you bide?'

A spark, as from a flint, that surprises me as much as them. 'A very fine house – sandstone's warmer than granite, don't you think? Traditional. A pleasant area of town, near the abbey. And if I remember rightly, a fine view of the sea.'

'And – did you advertise?'

'How well dae ye ken her, this maid?'

The voices already more curious than confrontational. 'Well enough.'

'You're no feart something micht gae wrong?'

'I've no fear of anything any more.' I see a shape on a page.

When little's left to hope for,

The less will be to fear.

'But… are you sure you're doing the right thing?' from the far end of the table.

'Does anyone ever know what the right thing is?' I scrape my ration of butter to the edges of my bread, with vigour. The soup's my favourite, lentil with bacon.

Feet shuffle under the table.

My mind's been everywhere but where it should be. As well Minnie took it on herself to come early. The trunk went on Tuesday with the carrier. She's talked to the doctor and the minister, finalised things with the hotel. Yesterday my lawyer approved the financial arrangements.

The train must leave soon.

It's never too late, they say – another chance for me to leave the past behind, to believe in miracles and mysteries… and I'm as jittery as if I'm embarking on a love affair.

Minnie's singing, I don't think she even knows she's doing it. She makes sure for the second time that my bags are secure on the rack. Out there on the platform, the world goes by. A couple wrap themselves round one another. A wave, a shout, and another pairing off. A toddler pulls at the hem of his mother's coat. Women fuss over hair, twist headscarves. One leans against a wall, looking at her feet. One checks a packet of Woodbine. A train pulls up at the next platform. People spill out, hurry away.

'I don't suppose I'll ever be back in Aberdeen.'

'Maybe aye, and maybe no, and maybe I suppose so. Never say "never", my mither aye said.' She's checking the tickets now. 'Mind, I'll maybe nae be back masell. It's a gey dour place.'

'But the granite fairly glints in the sun.'

She puts the tickets away again.

I don't know why it should, but the carriage door being slammed makes me lose my nerve. 'We cannae turn the clock back, Minnie.'

'No. But we'll keep oor fingers crossed.'

'I've been so long on my own.'

'I dinnae want nothin. Just you've tae pay yer board, that's all!'

A shout from the platform: a man runs past the window, his raincoat flapping. He climbs aboard. The door bangs just before the blast of the guard's final whistle. The engine draws the train through a cloud of smoke and steam.

'You take after your mother. She'd a lovely singin voice.'

'My mum? Did she?'

'Sang like a lintie…'

'Would ye credit that? My ain mither and I dinnae think I ever heard her sing.'

'The ballads, that was her thing. Her and Robert used tae sing at school concerts. The voice, she had, for all the size of her! You wondered where it came frae. I aye wished I could sing like her.'

'Well, but your poetry, that's your… what you're good at.'

'A poor imitation.'

'Everybody can sing.'

'No, no, lass. A pure voice, frae the heart, that's a gift. Without any words, it speaks to the soul, intoxicates you. Poetry, now… that's craft, a skill folk learn. The words lose something as they're pulled through the marrow o the bones. They might touch the soul, but they'll never hae that same power.'

The train's gathering speed. A dinghy's adrift on the river. There's a flutter of nerves in my stomach. 'What is it they say? "Haste hinders guid coonsel".'

'Maybe I should hae gien ye langer tae mak up yer mind?'

'No, no. I meant, I hope you won't regret what you've got yourself into.'

'Nae chance.'

The line skirts the coast. The tide's well out, the sea the colour of pewter. The ring on my finger slips easily over the knuckle. Back and forward, back and forward. 'Why do you never call yourself Williamina?'

'Mum aye called me Minnie.'

'Your grandfather, you'll be called after?'

'My Uncle Wull. I never kent him though.'

I straighten my coat across my knees. 'I met him.'

'At my gran's?'

'Maybe at a dance, sometimes, now and then – a great fiddler, he was. But I hardly knew him, really.' I fumble with the clasp of my handbag. 'I never really knew what he was like as a person.'

'Is the catch stiff?'

'A loner, I think.'

She takes my handbag and opens it. 'There!'

I stare at my purse, handkerchief, comb, compact, perpetual

calendar in leather case stuck at some point in the past. And my notebook.

'Is everythin all richt?'

'Fine. Thank you.' An express passes in the opposite direction. I close my eyes against the noise.

When I come to, Minnie's reading the People's Friend.

The landscape's familiar. 'The North Esk made a new course for itself, when I was a bairn.'

'That so?'

'Some night, it was. The tide on ae side o the dunes and the river on the other, and between them they forced a new channel though. Where the river used tae be, there was nothing but marshland.' She looks back, but we're amongst fields of barley now and the description means nothing.

The train stops at Montrose. She looks across the mudflats. 'My gran bade ower there.'

'Aye, Dun Estate.'

'Mrs Violet Jacob, the poet, comes frae The House o Dun.'

'Aye.'

'Dae ye think she'd hae kent my gran?'

'She did.'

'Really?'

'Your gran used to speak about her. You'll have read Mrs Jacob's novels?'

'And her poems. I like them.'

'You'll be invitin her to stay next?'

'Och, dinnae be sae daft!' The train teeters along an embankment. 'I dinnae think she'd hae kent my mum though.'

'Your mum was younger than her… and maybe a bit wild when she was a bairn.'

'Mrs Jacob would hae been posh.'

'Maybe so.'

The curve of a viaduct. A long way down children play in a patch of sand. I push my hand against the glass and close my eyes.

Minnie leans forward, touches my knee. 'You sure you're all richt?'

'Aye. Just, it's high bridges, above water. I never quite, you know… trust them. One of my friends was on the Tay Bridge that night…'

We rush headlong into a cutting. The print of my hand on the glass fades. 'Minnie, I want to be cremated.'

She presses a finger in the hollow of her neck, the way Cissy used to.

'These things have tae be talked about.'

'But no the day.'

'You'll see tae it, though?'

'Whit a woman!'

'And the ashes scattered on Elliot Sands.'

'Dinnae go sayin things like that! It's morbid.'

'No. It's just so nice to have somebody to tell.'

'Will ye nae get yersel settled in afore we speak aboot cairryin ye oot?'

'You're right,' – I nearly say Cissy – 'Minnie.' I lean over and catch her wrist: 'I get goose pimples, you're so like your mum!'

'Mum used tae say I was the image o Uncle Wull.'

'The Greigs were all alike.' My hat's tight against my brow.

'Ye're ower warm. Here, let me.' As she loosens the top button o my coat, the back o her hand brushes my chin. 'Sorry.' she says. 'I should hae done that sooner.'

I smile my thanks.

She's looking out at a sweep of sand.

'I walked hame from here once.'

'Tae Arbroath?'

'It was a fine night.' I jiggle the face of my watch though the hands will never move again. 'Soon be there. And I hope to goodness your employer is happy about this arrangement.'

'Ye're no gettin nae favours!' She tucks her hair behind her ear. 'My new mistress is gettin exactly what she wants, a lodger and a bide-in housekeeper. I tell ye, housekeepers are hard tae find – especially anes as guid as me. Aye, and so's the money tae pay them.'

'And you?'

'Me? I'm gettin a full week's wage for a half-time job – and that's nae tae be sneered at.' She counts on her fingers. 'Plus, I get a braw place to bide and, best thing ava, I get time wi you, at last.'

'I've aye thought o Arbroath as hame.'

'It's a wonder you and yer sister, aifter the war – the last ane I mean, nae this ane…'

'You mean the war to end all other wars?'

'Aye, well. But, I was thinkin, if ye'd bocht a wee hoose in Arbroath then…'

'Ethel didn't like Arbroath.' Minnie doesn't say anything. Perhaps I mumbled. There's no visible scar but I find the spot

– top joint, index finger, left hand. The skin's thicker and it's numb if I press. 'A new start, that's what we needed.'

'Am I mindin richt? Ye was doon Edinburgh wey, afore?'

'The Borders. My war service – if you can call it that – was in a POW camp. The recreation tent. It was all arranged through the kirk, of course. But oh dear! A dreary place in the winter.'

'Gey bleak in Arbroath tae.'

'Barren. God knows how the prisoners must've felt. Robert – pure chance, of course – he came to the camp, now and again.'

'Mr Cunningham?'

'Aye. Once or twice. Through the university, it was. Edinburgh University. Educational classes, they organised – and not just practical things. Languages, philosophy, history, botany, were all popular. Anything to take their minds off… we sometimes met in Hawick for tea.'

'Mr Cunningham and you? That would hae cheered ye.'

'It's comforting, a familiar face.' I smooth my gloves so they don't look as if my hands are still in them. I pull a loose thread and the thumb splits from the palm.

'I'll stitch that.' She studies the seam. 'Looks like a life-line, doesn't it? Look, that's you turnin for hame.'

'You read palms?'

'No, no. I dinnae ken whaur that came frae.'

The train slows as we pass the ruins of the abbey. 'Three-score years and ten, since I first arrived in Arbroath.'

The tide lapping at the turnpike road; a sign, "Brodie's Cooperage"; a great laden cart of stone. The processional entry to a ruined abbey, a forest of chimneys. Traces of salt on my lip; the smell of fish; a plunging red cliff; swirling, screeching sea birds.

'Ye wasnae born here?'

   'No, in Sunderland.'

   'Dae ye mind bein there?'

In the parlour, mama's sideboard. The smell of the blue drapes, the footstool that squeaked – rubbing my fingers on the spout of the lustre-ware teapot to see if the gold would come off.

   Outside, in the street, rounded cobbles underfoot, a sideways lurch, a straining of boot buttons: mama's hand held tight.

'I was always called "the little Scots lass". That's why coming to Arbroath felt like coming home.'

   The train pulls up at the platform. Minnie stands and reaches for my bags.

   'I just hope it's not too heavy a burden.'

   She opens the carriage door, sets the bags on the platform, comes back for me. Her hands steady me at the elbows. I let her take the weight, tilt my head back, draw the brine into my lungs.

   The gulls welcome me back.

CHAPTER 13

Arbroath: June 1945

He can see it's not a good time, but the very new minister at Erskine Kirk had heard I was in town. My father is a legend, he tells me. Himself, not an inspirational preacher, he'd be the first to admit it, but sincere. He couldn't wait to meet me – poetry is his passion.

The wheelchair Cissy begged from a friend in the Red Cross is comfortable enough but it's wide for the garden path and I feel awkward, her standing behind, him standing above me.

He wanted to suggest something, so I could mull it over. Wouldn't it be uplifting if we could start a Poetry Society? Would I be willing to...? He thinks the better of what he's about to say. Well, perhaps, if I could advise, recommend?

I thank him for coming and say I'll think about it. He wonders if we could talk sometime.

Cissy sees him to the garden gate and says she'll let the mistress know, out of courtesy, and get back to him with a time that'll be more convenient.

She's fussing a bit, all that happing and tucking. I tell her I'll be fine waiting here, and there's no need for a rug, it's a lovely day, and she can take the magazine away. There's better things to see here, in the sun and the fresh air and the scent o the carnations. Look at the bumble-bees all over them – and there, look at that! A blackbird tugs at a worm the length o the High Street. 'Do you ever wonder, Cissy...'

'I do that. I wonder if you'll ever get my name richt!'

'Oh, sorry, lass.'

'Dinnae be daft. Wonder what?'

It's gone right out of my head. 'Your mother was a lucky woman.'

'I dinnae think she'd much o a life.'

'She'd you.'

It's nothing to her, the touching. She'll hold my hand as we sit together in the evenings. At bedtime she coories in, just for a wee minute, when she kisses my cheek. At first it was an embarrassment, but... oh, the dear lassie persists, and now I've come to expect it. Skin on skin: that can be a comfort, can't it?

My throat catches and a tightness in the roof o my mouth makes it hard to swallow. The sound I make is more like a cry than a cough but it clears the tubes. I don't know where the tears come from but I push them back before they do any harm.

The man in the next garden pops his head over the dyke. He's pleased to meet me, expects to see more of me now summer's finally arrived. His wife's local, thinks I might have been her first Sunday school teacher, but it could have been my sister.

She doesnae come out much these days... is still grievin for the young lad that didnae come hame.

Minnie's back. She thinks it'll dae me the world o good tae get doon by the shore. Once she gets the hang of manoeuvring the chair and I get used to the way it veers to one side, I think it's a great invention. We take our time going through the park.

'We used to meet here.'

'Who?'

'Me, and Robert and your mum.'

'And Mrs Cunningham?'

'Aye, but that was later.'

'You must hae stories aboot my Mum. You'll hae tae tell me aboot how ye met, that kind o thing.'

Papa's gripping my hand so hard it hurts. I tuck myself behind him to escape from the salt spray and wish I could've stayed at home.

Someone shouts – another massive wave on its way! The people at the front push back. Shivering with fear or cold, I peer through the dusk. The top corner of the gable wall crumbles under the weight of sea-water.

I tell papa I want to go home.

He says at least I've got a home to go to. It hasn't just been washed into the sea. And if I think this is bad, well it's nothing compared with the other shores of the German Ocean. In Holland, miles of dykes have given way, great sea lakes are flooding the country, people and livestock have been drowned, hundreds of homes swept away and fields ruined.

The harbour master directs papa to the boat builder's shed. He bangs with his stick on the big double door. One side opens a crack, just enough to let us through. The smell of wood welcomes us. 'Wait there, Marion,' he says. Beneath the ribbed skeleton of a boat I imagine being swallowed by a whale.

Men stand in a huddle. A woman is hunched on a stool, one boy on her knee, one standing beside her. They all share the same blanket. At their feet, an oddly shaped bundle, a black kettle and a round-bellied pot. There's a girl, with bare legs and clogs on her feet, who looks as if she's ages with me. She's whistling 'Soldiers of the Queen', and inching towards me.

I can't whistle, but I can make some sense of things.

'Where will you go?' I wave in the general direction of my father, hoping she'll understand he can make things better. 'I mean, what are you going to do?'

The toddler sitting on her hip is shifted to the other side. 'Well then, what exactly would ye think we'll "do"?'

She doesn't seem at all put out. 'Sorry. I didn't mean... I thought that... it's just, was that your house?'

'Div I care?' She scuffs her feet through the sawdust.

A man hisses at her: 'Enough.'

'We'll get somewey else tae bide. That hoose stank o fish.'

Her words, my accent: I look away. The slap of a hand across her face startles me.

'Enough, I said. Less o the cheek, at a time like this. Damned lucky we were tae get that hoose, and dinnae you forget it.' The man's hand hovers.

My father's voice: 'Mr Greig, be assured, members of the church *will rally round.'*

'Be that as it may.'

The girl takes my arm and pulls me further away from the men.
'Didnae even hae linoleum on the flair,' she says in a low voice.
'I'm Cissy. Cissy Jean Greig. Dinnae mind my Da.'

'My name's Marion.' I whisper back.

'I ken. I've seen ye at the kirk.'

A rush of blood: 'You go to Erskine?'

'We're nae lang here, just like you.'

'Do you like Arbroath?'

'Nae much. But I'm gaein tae the High School.'

'You're going?'

'It's nae just for the likes o you, ye ken.'

I glance at papa but he's still talking. 'Sorry, I didn't mean...'

'You didnae mean this, you didnae mean that... well, what did
ye – bloody – mean? D'you think just because ye speak posh and
walk wi yer nose i the air ye're better than the rest o us? Let me
tell you somethin. Latin verbs is Latin verbs if ye speak English or
Scots and I bet I ken mair o them than you dae.'

Two of the little children start to cry. It's nothing to do with me
but it makes me want to cry too and what on earth have I got to
cry about?

Her elbow digs into my side. 'Dinnae be daft.' She shifts her little
brother to the other hip. 'Div ye nae ken I'm teasin? I can speak
lah-de-dah tae, ye ken. My mum worked for the gentry, the real
gentry, at a bigger hoose than you hae.' The little pinkie of her free
hand wiggles in my face. 'Would you like a cup of tea, my dear
miss?'

Papa hurries all the way home but it's easier with the wind in my back. I skip up the hill. He rings the house bell before he opens the door. I take off my outer clothes in the porch and unlace my boots.

'Wait here, Marion.'

The doctor's coming down the stairs.

I curtsey. 'I've a new friend,' I tell him.

They talk above my head.

'And a new baby brother,' father says.

'I doubt if I know anything you don't. The family came to Arbroath to better themselves – not Wull, he left home rather than come to work in the mills – and things didn't work out.'

'How come?'

I take a while to decide where to begin. 'When both the wee boys died, the family lost heart.'

'Scarlatina. I kent aboot that.'

'Then your granny's accident left her with a terrible sore back, and there was the trouble in the mill… they blamed your Grandad for that – stirring up the workers. Nobody would take him on then.'

'It's a wonder they didnae leave the toon.'

'I don't think they'd anywhere to go. Your grandad wanted Wull to come back, so your mum could stay on at school. But your granny – your mum too, I think – knew it wouldn't work. Your Grandad and Wull just didn't get on. But somebody had to keep the family together, so your mum took it on herself. And after that, she… well, it was probably as much our fault as hers.

We all just let things slide, I suppose, lost touch completely, in the end.'

'Must hae broken her hert.'

'She could've done anything, if she'd been able to stay on at school.'

'You think so?'

'Things were just beginning to change, for women.'

'Aye, but nae for workin folk.'

'Well… there might have been chances, for an educated woman. Some of us thought… lots of women wanted more of a say. But life isn't fair, is it?'

'Ye can say that again.'

'And she never married. Did she ever say anything about your father?'

'Never.'

'She was so popular, at school. Because of her spirit… you know what I mean? Could have had her pick. Just imagine what might have happened. Your mum liked Robert, you know. What if she'd married him? What a difference that would've made to your life.'

'My mum did the very best she could for me.'

'Oh, I'm sorry lass, I didnae mean any criticism.'

'It wasnae aye easy for her.'

'No. It can't have been.'

'Mr Cunningham wouldnae hae married her oniewey.'

'He liked her. I told you, they used to sing together.'

'I cannae think o naebody didnae like him. But he was… well, put it this wey. My mither was frae workin folk.'

'And what if I'd married Robert?' I don't know why I come out with that.

She treats it as a joke. 'By God, ye'd hae been a damned lucky woman, so ye would. But I dinnae think ye'd hae had much chance. Mrs Cunningham, she aince tellt me she'd aye kent he was the ane for her, frae when she was a wee lassie. He didnae aye ken it, she said, but... she'd hae scarted yer een oot for him.'

'You could be right.'

'Mr Cunningham – or Mrs – never said. Aboot him singin, I mean, wi my mither.'

'Maybe they didn't remember.'

The North Sea laps across the rock pavement of the bay. At Danger Point, it grinds and pulls at the shingle. There always was more of a breeze here. After more than half a century, a pile of rubble still lies on the shore.

CHAPTER 14

◠

Arbroath: June 1945

Black clouds in the distance are the only sign of the summer storm that kept me awake half the night. The early sun is making the south façade of the Abbey glow. Across the rooftops, beyond the harbour, beyond the links are the sands: golden today, instead of silver. The light is glancing off the sea the way it would off a mirror. I shade my eyes.

At breakfast the lady of the house wonders if – perhaps – it might be more convenient for me to entertain my guests in the sitting room upstairs.

I don't want to trouble her.

'It's no trouble.' She bites her bottom lip. 'But if you're receiving visitors… it's silly of me, but I didn't envisage… the sea air's done you such a world of good already, hasn't it?'

It's just that the upstairs sitting room isn't ideal – no table, and not a stick of decent furniture to be got in the town, even if she'd coupons left – which she doesn't, that's another problem. She wouldn't like people to think… 'But, my dear, what would you prefer?'

'There's such a lovely view from that window, and always something to watch on the sands.'

She hadn't thought of that.

And – I don't like to admit it – I've a tendency to get lost in my own thoughts. The memories crowd in on me and that's all the company I need. But really, whatever's the least inconvenience to her will suit me fine.

She rings the bell.

Minnie says the room'll be all the better for getting regular use. And there's that auld table in the back scullery that's just takin up space. Not a thing wrang wi it, a few scratches and a water mark. Yon bonnie chenille cloth in the linen cupboard would cover it fine.

She gets the nod.

Well then, here's another suggestion, if she micht be sae bold? It's a big enough table, wi the leaf up. And it'd fair save Marion's legs, if she was tae eat her meals up there.

'But you'd have to run up and down the stairs with trays of food?'

'Nothin tae me.'

'Three times a day?'

'The back stair.'

'I wouldn't like our guest to have to eat alone.'

'No, of course not.' She waits.

The lady of the house realises there might be some sense in it. If I really preferred to eat upstairs… what if Minnie ate with me, instead of in the kitchen by herself? When it fitted, of course, with her other duties.

I tell her she's most gracious. It'd certainly be easier on my legs and I wouldn't worry so about being late for a meal, or anxious when she's entertaining other guests.

'Let's give it a try.'

Cissy – I mean Minnie – winks at me as she leaves.

⁓

'I'll nae tell.' Cissy winks.

I say mama will not be at all pleased.

'God's sake, stuffy as a quilted hen, ye are. Even Miss Violet wasnae feart tae ploiter.'

'Well, go and play with Miss Violet.'

'I'll push ye in that water.'

'You wouldn't.' She's already picking her way across the slabs of rock coated with tiny mussels, like seal fur. I tear at my laces, throw my boots after her. 'Wait, Cissy!'

There's a warm light at the entrance, but the temperature drops sharply as we move into the shadow. The walls are smooth and damp. She shows me the engraved sailing ship. We speak in whispers, arms linked. I shiver.

'My Daddy taen a candle,' Cissy says. 'I forgot that.'

The rocks beneath our feet give way to gravel, then sand. The cave narrows into a passage. The darkness moulds itself round us. 'Ye're nae feart, are ye?'

'I've never been in a cave before.'

'It's nae a cave, it's a tunnel.' She puts on a quavery voice. 'And I'm the ghost o…'

The passage curves. I'm pulled to a sudden stop.

'What is it, Cissy?'

'Up there. Look!'

A glimmer, on the ceiling. 'Is it a reflection?'

'Oh! Thank God, we must be half-wey there.' We feel our way round the next bend, and my eyes adjust to the ligh. There's a wee bay, framed in the other entrance.

The sun's brighter this side, the water a different blue. Gannets launch themselves from ledges on the cliff-face that falls to a shingle beach. The air is still. 'There's nobody here but us!'

'Ach, easy! Ye must hae some gumption aifter aw.'

'There's no other way we could get here, unless we flew.'

'A smuggler's boatie.'

I wave my arms in the air and whoop and shout at seagulls and laugh and argue wi my echo and laugh even more. I paddle and chuck stanes and splash wi the flat o my hand and scoop up handfuls o water and throw them because these are the things Cissy does, and I can dae them too.

At last we sit watching distant white dots on the horizon dive for their supper. She tosses a handful of gravel into the air. 'I didnae even like Miss Violet. Wull and her aye left me ahent.'

'We'll be best friends.'

'Just the twa o us.'

'You'd like Robert too.'

'He's a toff.'

'He's fun, he dares you to do things – like climbing down the cliff.

I'm going to do that.'

She sifts through her list of insults and throws one at me. 'Stupid gowk.'

'You can come too, if you want.'

She sticks out her tongue.

'Cissy, what's gumption?'

'Just what ye need tae… get on wi things, if ye dinnae want tae be the snotter up some toff's nose aw yer days. I could hae got a job at Dun, ye ken, if I'd wanted it. A guid job.'

'You don't though, do you?'

'My daddy wants me tae stick in at the school. He says a lassie shouldnae hae tae look at her reflection in ither folk's siller for the rest o her life.'

Her head rests on my lap: she sings, quietly. 'I'll learn ye some, Minnie, if ye like – gumption. Then ye willnae need that Robert nae mair.'

CHAPTER 15

Arbroath: October 1945

'Nae much lather frae this soap.'

There's the ring of glass on porcelain, and the jug makes music as it fills. Water spreads its warmth across my skull. 'That good?'

I say it is but it's more the resting my head on the sink that helps.

'Anither rinse,' she says, 'and that'll be it. Move ower a wee bittie... there, that's grand.' She wraps my head in a towel, turban-style.

'Minnie.' A sore head's no excuse to put it off.

'What is it?'

'My brother-in law has an old-fashioned sideboard of mine. When we sold the house – Ethel and me – we got rid of the furniture, everything except for that. You ken what it's like, the kind o thing you feel attached to. Anyway, Amy said she'd keep it for me. Walter's probably never even looked in it since Amy died. I've a hat box, inside, with papers.'

'Poetry?'

'Well… unfinished stuff, maybe. And family things: photos, letters, certificates.'

'I could get them for ye.'

'They need to be destroyed.'

'If ye were tae write tae yer brother-in law…' she sees my face. 'Would ye like me tae dae that?'

'I don't suppose you'd… what about the sideboard? Would you hae room for that?' I shrug.

She says she'll ask.

'No, but I wondered if you… no, I dinnae suppose you'd like a thing like that?' I pull the towel closer round my neck. 'When I go, I mean. It's maybe too old-fashioned. It was mama's, you see.'

She makes a good job of mopping up the sink. 'I'm no doin this for what I can get.'

'No, but if I wanted you to have it? It's a fine piece.'

She helps me through to the sitting room and sets me in a chair at the window. The sun's too bright for my eyes. My hair is towelled until she's satisfied it's dry enough.

'It's just the minister, aye speaking about papa. I'm glad folk mind him that way, but I thought, what about mama? We didnae always see eye to eye, but in the early days… and whaur in the world would papa have been without her? She was aye there at his back, and naebody thinks of her at all. Who in the world will remember her when I'm gone? I thought… at least if you had the sideboard…'

Framed inside the two glass-panelled doors, tapestry: a young man holding out his hand to help two ladies over a stream. They're wearing crinoline dresses and elaborate wigs. The younger, in red and gold, is poised to step over. The older – in pale tones with silver accents – stands back a little. I trace the shape of the women with my finger. 'That's Amy' I tell papa, 'and that's Ethel.'

'And where are you?'

'The handsome prince.'

'You can't be a handsome prince. You're a girl!'

Well, I don't know where I am.

Papa says I'll be dreaming somewhere, and isn't it a pity there aren't two handsome princes.

Mama says I've left fingerprints all over the glass again.

Her hands rest on my shoulders. 'I'll keep it for ye, and gladly. But for God's sake dinnae think I need a sideboard – anything – tae mind me o you.'

'And Ethel. I've put her name put on the gravestone, but otherwise… there's nothing, is there?'

'Dinnae fret yersel. We'll speak aboot this the nicht. But for now, I'm sorry, I'll need tae awa and dae some work.'

'Aye, right enough. I'm fine. I'll just sit here, Minnie.'

'I dinnae suppose ye feel like writin the day? Now we've sic a braw table up, and naebody tae bother ye?'

William Souter said it better than anyone.

> *When the mind would speak*
> *But the heart has nought to say –*

Wait for the hour
Wait for the hour

'My hands are that stiff. I can hardly haud a pen.' Yet I feel the spread of the nib on the down-stroke, the hesitation at the turn, the easy slide of the up. I don't want to mention the head-ache.

'But ye could try. Just, ye've settled that well. And I thocht, if ye were happy, ye'd want tae write.'

It never was about a pen in my hand – that came later – or about happiness.

Something'd take my fancy. Then... a spark... an insight... inspiration, wonderment – call it what you will. I call it enchantment. Something I read, or saw; smelled, heard – touched! Something that made my blood quicken, my gut heave; that stiffened my backbone, narrowed my eyes, made my ears alive to nuances o sound, as I followed my whim, my desire, my urge – my need – to write, create. Everythin else pushed aside: nothin mattered but the power to scatter words on paper, to encourage them to find their rhythm, their pattern.

'I'd feel that proud – if I could encourage ye.'

Sometimes I'd read back what I'd written and wonder where it came frae. 'I've nothing much left to say, lass.'

'Och, but ye are happy here... are you nae?'

I think if she wants a happy endin she should write a fairy story, but that's maybe just the sore head speakin. Just being here, wi her, that'd be enough for me. Surely I dinnae have tae write it as well?

But. I remember... of course I mind what it is to be happy.

Words, words, words: they rattle around in my skull, making my headache worse. But still, they're safer in there. If they aren't said, no one can judge, argue; belittle, criticise, accuse, ridicule, condemn... It's just when you speak them – words – or write them, sometimes they mean something else to somebody else or you think they mean something and they don't quite mean that, or you give away something about yourself that you shouldn't because any normal person would... no-one would like to know something like that.

Or maybe you're an empty shell, and maybe that's worse than being bad, worse even than the pain in your head. Maybe you always have been, ever since... since

There's something wrong.

A voice like that never lies.

I want Minnie to know papa's here again but he's looking very stern and his finger is on his lips and that means I've not to say another word, not one, because... it's no-one else's business, is it?

That must be why Minnie's gone.

Has she gone? Has she really? I didn't think she'd... papa will stand by me. It's quite dark, just the flicker of his candle, and I'm not usually scared but something has a grip of my throat and won't let go.

I didn't think Minnie would leave... it must be my fault. Mama always said it was my fault.

She will come back. I know she will, And if she does, and if I get free, then maybe I can let her to know...for real – but then it's just how do you say it? Must I… is that the only way?

I try and I try again to reach out for her but papa's still in the way, and the flame of the candle on his tray dances, but makes no shadow. What was round my throat is twined all around me. I can't budge.

I can't breathe any more.

The headache's very, very bad. There's the sound of wind in my ears; fire in my lungs. My head sinks forward on my chest. I've broken out in a sweat but feel as cold as someone who never even knew how to love, and that's not true. I have loved. I have, I have. I have. I know I have.

There's something wrong.

Yet Cissy's better. She went back to school yesterday, papa told me that. And I'm much better. Just a few days ago the rash covered me from head to toe and I was so ill I didn't care.

The redness has gone. I'm not too hot. My tongue doesn't feel as if it's choking me. I can open my eyes wide and the light doesn't hurt. The flakes of skin I pick from my arm are like pieces of lace.

Just a headache, that's all that's wrong. Just a headache. And George isn't crying today – he must better too. Just in time for his first birthday. I'll give him a big hug and a cuddle and bring him into my bed and tickle him and whisper I'm sorry.

But something's wrong.

My legs wobble when I slide out of bed. I hold onto the dressing table and make it to the door then have a rest before I cross the landing to the top of the stairs. The bannister helps me down. I'm following muffled sounds from the parlour. In the hall I lose

*control of my legs, then my body starts to shake. I fall against the
door just as papa opens it.*

*He catches me. 'Marion, come and pray with us.' With him
supporting, I walk into the parlour. Mama's face is very red.
George is wrapped in his white shawl.*

'For our baby, George. God bless his soul.'

*He doesn't like being wrapped in a shawl. He likes to think he's
as big as Cissy's little brothers – God bless their souls.*

*Mama's swollen eyes stare at me. She told me to stay away from
that girl, didn't she? Didn't she?*

*Papa comes between us, but she pushes him away. Didn't she?
Didn't she? Didn't she? She pulls George's shawl away from his face
and thrusts him at me. Didn't she?*

There's a blow to my head, and a smell, like burning rubber,
in my nostrils. Papa's gone and baby George is beckoning. He
always smiles like that when he sees me! He's holding out his
arms... his skin is luminous, his head – pointed, I'd say. He
looks about six years old.

I'm so happy he grew, even though it was just a little bit.

Pincers grip the back of my head. The rhythm of the pain is...

> *This ae nichte, this ae nichte,*
> *This ae nicht and alle*
> *Fire and fleet and candlelight*
> *and Christ receive thy saule.*

Minnie's crying so that's good, she must've come back after all.

I'd like to stay with her and tell her all about George but it's such a long time since I saw him and he wants me to go with him. I can't let him go all by himself.

I hear Minnie tell me she loves me, and pause, for just a second, to look back.

I'd tell her, if I could, an artist would make something of this, capture with a few deft lines the way she's cradling someone's head, stroking hair from a brow, lifting a hand to her lips.

George isn't smiling now. I'm scared.

CHAPTER 16

Arbroath: November 1945

Cissy's face is so tight and drawn… since I came to Arbroath I've given her so much trouble, the dear girl.

She's scuttling along the kerb, trawling faces. I see her over the heads of the crowd and reach across to get her attention. 'Cissy!'

'It's yersel.' She's weighing me up.

'I didnae expect tae see you here.'

Enough of a sound to tell me she doesn't care what I expected, but she elbows her way through the crowd anyway and climbs on the doorstep beside me for a better view. 'Hae ye seen Robert?'

The sound of the band at last: all heads turn down the High Street. 'Robert?'

'Hae ye seen him or no?'

'No.'

She knows there's something I'm holding back.

The band's marching down the street now with the pipes

screeching and the crowd is shouting and clapping, so there's no point in saying more. The Right Honourable Member and his wife follow in their chaise. The Provost and the Town's Officers walk behind, a surge of children in their wake. Everyone jostles for an inch of space. Cissy pushes away from me, through the crowd. I feel my bodice much too tight.

When the procession has passed and the road clears, I slip away by Springfield. From the top of the bank I see the whole expanse of the park. Robert's size makes him stand out from everyone else.

'You got away.'

'Aye.'

'See anybody?'

I shake my head.

He gestures with his head. 'The cliff path?'

We walk together, apart.

∾

Everything's suddenly quiet and still, peaceful. But I don't quite know where I am. I do know this is not where I should be. If only I could remember where… it might be the sands. I think that's where I've to go. And if I don't go now, it'll be too late.

I avoid the tread that squeaks, tiptoe across the hall, ease the door handle round and the door back into place.

The sun's just clearing the horizon. The air's chilly, but I expected that. My shawl's tucked in the way Nellie taught me. A heron lifts itself out of the mist that lies low over the Keptie Pond – flies away, unhurried.

A moment's hesitation, then I hitch up my skirt and take the old path across the park, watching my feet, jumping bramble bushes, keeping my balance despite the slope. I'm winded when I get to the old wooden dolphin. A coal cart trundles by, a woman fills a pail of water in the courtyard of the Signal Tower, three fishing boats slip into harbour. A thread of workers snakes towards Mill Street. The dolphin's back is smooth and warm to touch.

I cross the links to the beach, getting my feet soaked with dew. The sandbank's cushioned with sandwort, thistles and sorrel. Two crows stop bickering long enough to check me over.

Where the Elliot Burn sinks into the sand, I stop and look back at my footprints that are faint as the tracks of sandpipers. I didn't mean to come this far.

A figure crossing the links makes me start. I don't want to see anyone, not even to say 'Good morning'. I stumble through the softer sand near the wreck, to hide under its hull. I'm about to duck under when Robert jumps out and wrestles me onto the sand.

'You've come!'

'Stop it, Robert. Let me up!'

He rolls off. 'But I thought, when I saw you…'

'I didn't expect you to be… you shouldn't have come.'

'Hell, Marion, I've been coming here since I was a boy. It was me that brought you here in the first place.' He pulls me to my feet. 'Damn it, lassie, well what do you want?'

'I love this place. You know that.'

'Nothing to do with me?'

'It's just that… everything is on the edge here: the sands meet the sea and the sea meets the sky, and the sky rests on the tops of the dunes. Everything's natural, as it should be. Everything cyclical. Everything merges.'

'Christ, if in doubt write a bloody poem.' He waves to the figure on the sands. 'Look,' he says, 'here's Cissy.'

'Cissy? What's she doing here?'

'What's it to you?'

⌒

From the bed I can just see thick grey cloud out the great window at the end of the ward, but it's easy to imagine the sea and the sands. The nurse is tidying up for Matron's afternoon round. 'It's going to thunder,' she says.

'It's going to thunder.' The pine bark is rough against my back. A field of marigolds stretches to the sea. Margaret's green silk is much too formal for a country walk.

'Go back then.'

'I'm not leaving you.'

'Is that what they said? "Don't let her out of your sight."' I draw on my cigarette.

She makes a bud with her lips. 'I always thought you quite liked me.'

I make a show of being all ears.

'Damn you, don't make fun of me.'

... five, six, seven, eight... 'My mood has nothing to do with what I think of you.'

'At least now you admit you're in a mood! Why won't you talk to me? It's not my fault.'

'Nor mine.'

'You're the one who turned him down.'

'And guess what... you're the one who's an unwanted "companion".'

The clouds are blowing in from the Channel at a rate of knots.

'Well, bad luck for you.'

Being angry suits her. 'God's sake, Margaret, just let me be.'

She gazes past me into the wood.

'And you need to let Robert be. Don't you understand that?'

'Robert and I are and have always been good friends.'

'You can't just keep pretending. He'll always adore you. He'd do anything for you. You need to step back, give him a chance... give some other woman a chance.'

'He doesn't even like poetry.'

An intake of breath: 'Well, he'll be a good catch for someone, if you ever let him out of your clutches. But Marion, quite apart from all that business, I did think that, coming here with you, we'd have a chance to... You know, after you and Cissy – whatever happened between the two of you, it's none of my business, I don't want to know – I don't need to know. But I hoped that maybe we'd become closer.'

Maybe I haven't been very fair to her. 'Look, Margaret, it's going to pelt. We need to shelter.' I slip an arm round her waist and part the branches with the other. We go deeper into the wood.

❧

I've been turning over so many things, so many memories, thoughts. Things I might have said, shouldn't have said, might have done, shouldn't have done, might still do, if I'm lucky – with the Grace of God, as papa would have said. Accepting there are things I can never do, things I can never say.

Forgiving, forgetting.

Knowing you might've gone, knowing this might be your last chance – that fairly concentrates the mind. You even come to accept the things you'll never ever understand, though you were to go over them and over them for eternity.

This could be my last chance to breathe in the reek of the smoke barrels, the mixture of tar and brine that is the harbour. Fishing boats and square-rigged brigs; fishwives loading their baskets, stevedores heaving rolls of sailcloth. The water in the harbour's flattened by the freezing fog: just a slight swell visible under the surface. The tide eases itself over boulders embedded in sand – a sound like the flap of stretched linen on bleaching poles.

East Grimsby – a jumble of coal merchants, chandleries and taverns. I tuck it all away and turn at the boat builder's yard.

In Canada I'll surely miss the smells of the High Street: the whiff of paraffin from Archie Stewart's close; bread and hot mutton pies; spices, cheese, tea, coffee, bacon, tobacco, vinegar. Towards the Abbey somebody's making marmalade. The warm stench from the stables: stale beer when someone opens the door of the public house on the corner of James Street, where Cissy lives.

Slates are missing from her roof. There's a crack in the window and the door's been splintered where someone has kicked it. I take my glove off for a sharper knock.

'Wha's that?'

I'm about to cry 'It's me, Cissy,' just like I used to, when the door opens.

She's wipin her hands on a peenie. Grey hairs already; her face still bonnie, but a gap in her teeth. The eyes still pierce me. 'Christ, you've a brass neck.'

I want to ask if she minds sharin a pennyworth o toffee and a bottle o ginger beer frae Stumpy Bowman's? My feet gettin tangled in the skippin rope; hide and seek in the kirkyaird; followin the burn in Tarry Den; scrunchin our taes in the sand? Does she mind climbin on the wooden dolphin? Pickin buckies frae the rocks?

My hand falls by my side. 'Cissy.' *I hesitate.* 'I think Wull micht hae spoken tae ye?'

'And if he has?'

'I really wanted tae talk tae you...'

'Ye never was backward at comin forward.'

'I'm sorry, Cissy, about... what came between us.'

'Atween us?' *She lets her mouth hang open.* 'Us?'

'I ken whit you think.'

'Mair than I dae, you bletherin shite.'

'I wish we hadnae lost touch over it.'

'And dae ye think it's made a whit o difference tae me? I've never gien the bastard anither thocht.'

'He didnae ever mean tae mak ye think...'

'Oh, aye, just wanted his cock up my drawers, did he? Because you wouldnae let him?'

It takes my breath away. For Wull's sake I stand my ground and narrow my eyes and find the strength to brush it off.

'Anyway, that's all over. You'll hae heard...'

She obviously hasn't.

'Margaret and him are gettin engaged.'

'Oh aye, is that the latest tittle-tattle at the soirées? And you thocht I'd be interested?'

'All I wanted was tae shake hands wi ye Cissy. For auld times sake. And for Wull. It was just, when I met him, it was like, fate. I thought it was meant. You know, the way Nellie used to talk?'

'Christ Almighty, dinnae bring Nellie intae it. Awa ye go, back whaur ye came frae. Ye didnae bide awa near lang enough. I tellt Wull ye were a hertless bitch.'

'Ye've seen him?' I can't help myself reaching out. 'Is he here already?'

She's shakin her heid.

'Hae ye heard from him though?'

Hands on her hips: 'Christ, I cannae mak sense o you. Whit would ye expect? Wull was in a bloody foul mood when I last saw him, and he's lang gone.'

'Gone? What dae ye mean?'

'Whit's it tae you?' She spits at my feet. 'Ye wasnae thinkin ye could leave oor Wull i the lurch and then pick things up again? Is that whit ye're here for? Surely even you wouldnae be sae daft, ye stupid bitch. Christ, I willna waste guid words. Get yersel oot o here.'

' *I dinnae understand you, Cissy.*'

'*Ye think I care? Ye think I care aboot you? Not a whit.*' *She shuts the door on me.*

It opens at a crack. '*God help his poor wife. It's her I've aye been sorry for.*'

'*His wife?*'

She takes her time to spell it out. '*Oh, ye didnae ken that, did ye nae? Fancy that, and you sae smart! Aye, his wife. The lassie maybe didnae hae the bittie paper, but my God she's put up wi mair shite frae my brither than you hae in ye. And that's saein something.*'

CHAPTER 17

Arbroath: January 1946

Everything seems clearer now. Waiting here for Minnie to take me home – again – I think it's not just the nursing care that has made me better. It's something in me… I've confounded them, and myself, too.

I watch the late afternoon sun light the underside of streaky clouds over the sea. The old wreck long gone.

And Minnie. She pulled me through. I'll tell her, soon. But for now – I can wait. Things turn out the way they're meant to be.

Robert's given up foraging for new specimens. 'God-forsaken place,' he's saying. 'You're right about the stone though. Impressive.' He estimates the height of it with the palm of his hand. 'Twice as big as I am' – spread-eagles himself.

'And wider than you can stretch.'

'A riddle without an answer.' He leans against the stone and pulls me into his arms. I feel with my foot for a tussock to stand on.

A slant of light. 'There are theories,' I tell him. 'The stones mark forces, powerful forces – magnetic – that shaped the earth.'

His expression warns me.

'But you'll know all about ley-lines.'

'Not a jot of scientific evidence, of course.' He moves across to touch the stone. 'Pure speculation.' Close into it now, he scans the surface from side to side, base to top. 'Jesus.' He half falls, half stumbles back.

I stretch out an arm to help him balance.

'Jesus, Marion, I thought the thing was going to fall on me.'

'It's the way the clouds are moving.'

'Jesus.' He leans his forehead against mine.

'A guilty conscience, that's what it is.' I trace a symbol on the surface of the stone. 'But Robert, what if – maybe our ancestors knew something we don't. Maybe through the stones they could tap into... what? Energy? Whatever it is. Draw on some invisible power?' There's a depression under my fingers that might be part of the pattern or might be a random carving by wind and rain. 'It's not so far-fetched.'

He gives me a hooded look. 'This is far-fetched. This war, bringing us together again. What are we going to do?'

'Maybe the evidence is there but we can't understand it.'

∽

An unexplained stop in the middle of an empty landscape. The windows are steamed up. There's a foustie smell in the carriage – damp greatcoats. The two soldiers in the middle seats are reading.

The ones near the door are staring at their boots.

'Let me see,' Robert mouths.

I shake my head.

He taps a finger on his chest. 'About me?'

I shake my head again, but he doesn't believe me. He takes out his diary and pretends to study it.

I hold my notebook even closer to my eyes. My writing's tiny, to economise on paper, and the light isn't good. That's nearly twenty years since I started and four years since I picked it up again. I flick through the pages and know I'm no further forward.

Matthew Chapter VII

1. Judge not, that ye be not judged.

6. Give not that which is holy unto the dogs, neither cast ye your pearls before swine, lest they trample them under their feet, and turn again and rend you.

Ticht buds, tinge o green on white
the seasons o love
painful pleasure

The full moon
lichts the nicht
and dances raindrops dew drops
on the thorny black
Makin pearls
o sic a bonnie sheen

Amid that darkened bush
Like faerie folk he fashions a ring o pearly hue
that binds me tae him aye (and gies it tae his love)
But doesnae gie his hert

The breeze… the blackthorn bush
(It's tune was) Its moanin better company than nane

Ayont the bonnie braes o (Angus) hame
Whaur wolves and thochts roamed free
The (Some) moonlicht (fell) (danced) tinkled frae the sky
and fair enchanted me.
It landed on (the blackthorn) a thorny bush
Wi a hert (as) black as (coal) the nicht
And blessed (its thorny hert) my weary een
Wi sic a bonnie sicht.

(The) (For) D(d)ew drops (covered them wi) (gied) lent (them)
(sic) a (bonnie)rainbow sheen
(and) when the (By the time the) sun rose in the sky.
(Like blossom on a tree.)

An eagle soared and lent his wings (tae)
and lifted me up high (no, no, no!!!)

On the bonnie (braes o hame)? There's ither bonnie braes
(In)(sterner company) and sterner company
(I learn) The lesson (is) mine tae learn (Rubbish!) and lessons

that (I hae tae learn) are meant for me
Thae pearls (forever) (are) aye in my mind)
'Pearls are for tears, you'll (find) see.'

Ayont the bonnie braes o hame
(In sterner company) all weary and alone
(The) A breeze (that) makes the thornbush (sing) moan
Is sterner company
I hear the thornbush moan 'pearls are for tears, you'll see.'
'Pearls are for tears' it moans

Ayont the bonnie braes o hame
My life began anew
When (my) true love (showed me) fashioned me a ring
wi beads o pearly hue.
(thae) (pearls) o sic a bonnie sheen they had
a tinge o green on white
I had nae mind o prickly thorns,
or (And) the blackness o the night.

Tak heed
speak your need

Ayont the bonnie braes o hame
Clad in mists and memory
My true love set me on a track (the road)
Towards Infinity.

Sometimes things just don't work out and you've to walk away. But sometimes you just have to keep faith.

The train starts again... stops within minutes at a station that's hardly more than a signal box. More moorland, then the odd farmhouse, fields, already ploughed, a village, a town that's still asleep. And at last the suburbs, but they seem to go on forever.

Robert's looking at my reflection in the window. I turn a little. He opens his mouth to speak. I shake my head just enough for him to notice.

When the train pulls into the station he takes my case down from the rack, but to anyone else he's just being helpful. He gets off first and holds his hand out to help me down, doesn't let go. The crowd moulds round us like water round an obstruction. 'It's over, Robert.' I grip the lapels of his jacket and bury my face in the tweed. 'Over. Over. Over.'

~

I'm waiting for Minnie, my back against a stone. Bracken fonds push through the debris o the auld year. A buzzard wheels above: far below, a slow sweep of figures across a field – the occasional flash of sun on sickle blades. Grasses whisper in my ear.

Robert, a faded deerstalker on his head, strides across the horizon. He sees me, veers in my direction, crouches in the shadow of the stone to pick a flower, holds it out to me, keeping his eyes on it. 'Linnaea Borealis.'

I cup my hand.

He lays the stem on my palm.

'It's bonnie.'

His hand catches my wrist. 'Like you are…'

I warn him off.

Eyes wide, he puts a hand across his mouth – mock horror. 'No, don't worry. I won't do anything silly. It's just… I'm pleased to see you. We both are. It makes Margaret happy to have you here.'

The flower is limp already: 'It's so fragile, Robert.'

'But it endures. Survives in the wilds, alone, unseen. Thrives in the shade.' Two crows skraik as they chase the buzzard. 'You won't say anything, will you?'

'No.'

'I know you won't.' He gestures at my book. 'And you're not going to spout poetry at me, are you?

CHAPTER 18

✁

Arbroath: March 1946

I manage everything but the buttons and totter across to the stool. Grey tones are the only colour in my face but they're a healthier shade of gray. Nothing I can do about the cow's lick that exasperated mama, the eyebrows that always make me look surprised, the wee scar on my chin from that time I fell on the rocks.

I used to sit on a stool as mama brushed my hair – she did like to do it, when I was wee. There was a little box on her dressing table – a picture of a forget-me-not on it, and the first verse I ever loved.

> *No earthly change will alter me,*
> *Whate'er may be my lot*
> *My heart will still be true to thee*
> *Then oh, forget-me-not.*

In the wing mirrors of the dressing table perfect copies of me disappear into infinity. Minnie, Marion. Daughter. It was only later it dawned that papa would've preferred a son, mama some more biddable daughter... it might not have cost me too much, to please her. Might have saved some heartache.

Sister: could've done better there.

The brush is too heavy but I can still draw the comb through my hair.

In-valid, but alive.

Friends. I've had friends, loved them, outlived them. Had lovers... didn't love them all, though must've needed something they offered. Could've been a wife, but doubt I'd ever have made a good one.

Poet? I might have been considered a poet once. Or shall we say 'poetess'. Shall we? And tinkeress? Tailoress? Soldieress? Sailoress?

At least I – me, myself – the real me, not one of these perfect images, might have done something worthwhile, once in a while... in a manner of speaking.

Might still.

Or maybe not.

No need to focus on myths of happiness when I can sit here and look out at the sea and the sky. I've lived, haven't I? Isn't that enough? If I haven't walked on water, I've walked on the earth. That's miracle enough.

The present is the only thing that can be taken from me now. And when I die, I'll lose exactly what George lost, no more, no less.

Minnie's calling to someone as she comes up the stairs, thinkin we've seen the back o the frost at last. She's early today. I put the comb down and make sure I'm sitting straight. There's a rap at the door and in she comes with a wee bunch of flowers, and her face is such a picture I'm glad I made the effort. 'Oh my!' She stops in her tracks. 'Ye're up? Ye've done it yersel!'

I hold out my cuffs so she can do the buttons.

'Well, done!'

'I'm feelin grand, lass.'

'Look, I picked ye some winter jasmine.'

'You're that guid to me.'

She lets me push myself into a standing position. 'As guid as new. Ye'll be oot in that gairden in nae time.'

'You go first.' I'm that determined to show her I can do it. She keeps looking back but lets me shuffle along the lobby at my own speed. I follow her into the sitting room and ease myself into my chair.

'My, but ye've done well.'

The table's set, the teapot waiting. She stirs it with a teaspoon, taps the spoon on the cup. 'Aye,' she says, 'and are ye nae wonderin what my letter is?' She points to an envelope propped against the milk jug.

'I didnae notice it.'

'I hope ye dinnae mind. Just a wee surprise. I didnae want tae tell ye till it was all arranged.'

Blairgowrie
27th February 1946

Dear Miss Greig,

Thank you so much for your kind words about my
poetry and for your invitation to meet Miss Angus.
I'm so glad to hear she's recovered from the little stroke
she had. I'd love to meet you both, and I'm quite able
to travel, thank you, though, like Miss Angus, I'm not
quite as sprightly as I once was.

I do remember your family. I knew your father well
when I was a child. After the family left Dun I got news
about him now and again – but nothing for a long
time.

I very much look forward to meeting you both
at Hayshead House at 2.00 o'clock on Thursday 9th
April. I'm hoping for a lovely spring day. I'm going
to ask my driver to bring me via Lunan – a bit of a
detour, I know, but Lunan Bay was a favourite haunt
of mine when I was a child and I just can't resist the
opportunity.

Yours sincerely
Violet Jacob (Mrs)

CHAPTER 19

⁓

Arbroath: April, 1946

The clock chimes the hour. Minnie checks I'm tidy. 'She'll be here any minute.'

'The letter was friendly enough.'

'A bit raivelled though. She'll hae meant my Grandad.'

'Surely.' The doorbell rings. 'Are there crumbs on my chin?'

She shakes her head. 'I'll get the door.'

I make it to the top landing in time to see Minnie straightening her collar and saying how pleased she is.

'I trust Miss Angus is well?'

'Aye, thank you, kindly,' Minnie says, 'Recovered very well.' She looks up. Mrs Jacob's eyes follow. I risk a hand off the banister to wave. 'How do you do.'

'How do you do. Pleased to meet at last.'

'Marion doesnae manage the stairs very well yet. You winnae mind gaein up?'

'Not at all. I'll take my time, that's the only thing. I walked further than I meant to at Lunan.'

'I envy you that!' I call down.

Half-way up the stairs she pauses, looks up to see how much further.

'I could come down, Minnie' I call. 'I think it's too much for Mrs Jacob.'

She leans against the banister. 'How silly of me to tire myself out.' Her face is pale.

'Why don't I come down?'

'My God, Marion, bide whaur ye are!' Minnie's helping Mrs Jacob to sit on the landing.

'Just breathless. I'll be all right.' Her head hangs forward.

'Ye need a doctor?'

She shakes a hand. 'No, no. No fuss.'

'We'll call your driver back.' Minnie says. 'I could catch him. You can come anither day.'

She wipes her brow wi the back of her hand. 'Oh dear, no. A wet cloth, please, that's all I need. And a minute's rest.' Looking up at me she adds: 'What d'you think? Is this our last chance?'

'Unless you come to my funeral?'

'I'm rather of a mind to carry on.'

I suggest we have tea on the landing. It'd be a shame to waste Minnie's scones.

'Splendid!' She's recovering. 'But… I've an even better idea.' She holds out a hand for Minnie to help her up. 'I don't suppose you keep whisky, by any chance, for emergencies? D'you know, I think a sip would do me – maybe all of us – the world of good.'

'I say that would get us off to a grand start.'

'Your colour's comin back, right enough.' Minnie looks relieved.

'I'm coming up. Miss...'

'Marion. Call me Marion.'

∽

We talk about the advantages and disadvantages of living in Kirriemuir and Arbroath, the war, the cost of living, rationing, everybody's business written down from cradle to grave. We thank God life's getting back to normal, though who knows how long it'll take, and things'll never be the same again.

'I lost my son in the first war,' Mrs Jacob says. 'The Somme.'

'A terrible waste of lives.'

'I couldn't talk about it, not for a long time.'

Minnie fills the gap. 'Your poem though... that was very sad.'

Mrs Jacob – Violet – likes the subtlety of my poetry, she doesn't think she had that touch, herself. 'And you write in a very natural Scots voice,' she adds.

I can't claim to be a native speaker, though sometimes I think there are two different folk inside my skin and they don't even speak the same language. But at least I know what the language should sound like. Somebody like Charles Murray catches it perfectly in his poetry, but to my ear a lot of what passes for Scots these days...

'Aye, well, MacDiarmid... but he's a giant of a character, isn't he? And his work...'

'Clever, isn't it?'

She won't be drawn. 'Scots came naturally enough to me. I was educated at home, you see and… I know it's not what you would expect, but my parents were so often away – sometimes I didn't see them for months. And almost all the servants spoke Scots. Then, of course, I often played with the children in the cottar houses.'

Minnie would have said something then but Violet minds something that makes her smile. We could have a wee duet, the two of us, she says. Isn't it ridiculous what some critics came up with? Did I ever read that review, the one that said my poetry was like a melody of the fiddle, hers the pianoforte?

My fiddle's been out of tune for a long time.

'One does rather get out of the way of things.' An awkward pause, then she asks what I think of the new T.S. Eliot.

We agree, and disagree. She bows to my superior knowledge of literature. I acknowledge her greater experience of life.

Minnie thinks she should leave the two of us. We surely willna miss her for a wee while?

'Oh please sit down, Miss Greig – sorry, Minnie – if you're free. You don't mind, Marion, do you?'

It's easier to make an appropriate gesture than say anything.

'I want to talk to you about your family. You getting in touch brought back such happy memories. I knew your grandparents well.'

'Aye, that's what I thought you meant, in your letter – my grandad.'

'He could turn his hand to anything, especially anything to

do with horses. He'd stand at the corner of the field and whistle and the horses would trot to him. And your grandmother... well, I suppose I knew her better than I knew my own mother. Just a week after I was born there was some problem with my nursemaid – I don't know what it was – some spectacular mis-understanding with the housekeeper, I believe. Anyway, she walked out. But Wull had been born a few weeks before me, so your grandmother just moved Wull over and fed both of us. Thought nothing of it, apparently.'

'Really?' Minnie's face a picture. 'Well, I never kent that. I never kent my gran, of course.'

'Remarkable woman. Fine looking – handsome – and a nice way with her. Just as at home at the big house as she was in her cottage. Any visitors we had, she was called in for a bit of fortune telling. Quite a reputation she had, amongst the gentry.'

'Fortune-tellin?'

'She'd a glass ball. I think it was actually just a fisherman's float, but she could see things in it.'

'Well, I never!'

'And cards. She could read the cards. Just an ordinary pack. Probably didn't need any prop actually– she'd that fleck in her eye.'

'Fleck?'

'Some say it shows the second sight. But I don't think your grandfather approved. She probably earned... I don't know for sure, but I believe people could be very generous.'

'My mum never ever tellt me.'

'I always wanted to be one of the Greigs, when I was wee. I

wanted to talk like them and dress like them and eat with them and play, of course.'

'And you kent my mum?'

'Well, yes, I did.' She looks a bit taken aback.

'But you and Wull were closest,' I say.

Her face opens up. 'Wull! My hero. I followed him everywhere. Helped him bring in the poultry – that was one of his jobs. And gather the eggs. He could smell out where they were. Once – I was maybe six or seven – I brought him into the big house to try my rocking horse. He pretended he wasn't interested, but then made it go so fast we both fell off. He got his behind leathered for that.'

'Hardly his fault.'

'No, it wasn't fair, but his father thought he should've known better.'

'You must have missed them – the Greigs – when they left.'

'The mills enticed so many folk off the land. But yes, I did. Wull especially. These were simple, happy days. Lying in a field of grass, looking up at the clouds, that was happiness.'

'But the cottar houses must have been dark and damp.'

'And full of draughts in the winter. And people had to collect water from the well; everything was black with coal dust; milking in the early hours of the morning… it was a hard life, no getting away from it. Mice and rats, of course, but you expected that, in the country. But the picture in my head, Minnie, is of your Grandad, on a Saturday night, in front of the fire – the Bible and the Burns book out. A great one for education, he was. Cissy and Wull – and me, sometimes, taking turns to read, in front of the fire – what a heat it gave out. The wee ones would be asleep in the box bed, the candle would flicker in the old stable lantern – it was like a little house with a metal roof – holes pierced in it – glass on three sides and a snecked wooden door on the other.'

'Lots o good things must hae been swept awa wi the bad.'

'He loved the land, your grandfather. It wasn't so much to work in the mill, that wasn't why he moved to Arbroath. He thought there'd be more chances for his bairns in the town… never got over Wull turning his back, going to live amongst his mother's folk. From what I've heard, anyway.'

'His mother's folk?'

'The Tinkers.'

Minnie stands up and walks across to the window, turns to speak but doesn't know what to say.

'I'm sorry, didn't you… I assumed you knew. She was proud enough of it.'

'Why would my mother never hae tellt me that?'

'People can be cruel.'

'But what's the disgrace in it?'

'None. Just, Tinkers didn't have the same place in the towns, and thanks to the new agricultural machines there was less and less for them to do on the farms. So, I suppose, they lost their place in society.'

I ask if she'd seen any of the Greigs after they left Dun.

'Never. Strange, isn't it, how people disappear from your life? I heard about them though. Wull had friends amongst the staff. Now and again he got a bed in the stables – wasn't the only one,

I'm sure. Even after I married and left home, I still occasionally got news. And there was the baby of course, that was a great to-do at the time.'

'Baby?'

She shakes her head. Her voice changes as she turns to Minnie. 'And are you musical, my dear? Wull was such a great fiddler. I think he loved his fiddle more than anything.'

'Nae me. But I hae the fiddle.'

'So that's where it went!'

'And she can sing,' I say, 'like Cissy.'

'Cissy had a beautiful voice, even when she was a little lass.'

'My mum used to sing at school concerts.'

'Cissy was in my class at school,' I say.

There's a pause. 'Ah...' Violet leans forward and pats Minnie's hand. 'Now I understand. Sorry, I thought for a moment you were meaning your real mum.'

Minnie frowns. 'She was my real mum.'

'But... oh, I didn't realise. I assumed, you see, you were Wull's child.'

I'm trying to think of things from Minnie's point of view. She's hiding her confusion well.

'No, Wull was my Uncle. My dad was... I never kent him. I think he died. My mum wouldnae talk aboot it.'

Violet's sitting right back in her chair. 'So let me get this right...'

'Cissy Greig was my mum. She died wi the flu, in the epidemic, at the end o the war.'

'You're Cissy's daughter?'

Minnie nods.

'So whatever happened to Wull's baby?'

I'm glad they've forgotten about me. I hardly dare to move.

'I didnae ken he had a baby.'

'Nor did he, that was the thing! It was after he went to South Africa.'

Beads of sweat on my brow: I mop them with a handkerchief and hold it tightly in the palm of my hand.

'I didnae ken he was in South Africa. And I dinnae think my mum kent that, but I suppose… she could hae. She just didnae speak aboot thae things.'

'The Boer War. That's where he went, enlisted.'

I push my hands under my thighs to stop them shaking. 'Oh dear God!'

'You all right?'

They're both looking at me now, expecting an answer. 'The Boer War!' I know I should stop, but my thoughts tumble out. 'That poor woman.'

'Woman?'

'My mum, you mean?'

'No, Minnie. His wife, I mean.'

'Oh no! It wasn't his wife's baby! I believe he did have a wife once, according to their own customs. But it wasn't her baby.'

'Look, I think ye'd better slow doon… that's if ye dinnae mind. Ye've fair lost me,' Minnie says. Who was his wife?'

'This is just from what I've gathered. When he was still very young, fifteen, maybe, not long after he left home, he ran away with a Traveller girl, someone his own age, possibly younger.

But her family never took to him. I don't know enough about it to say for sure, but I guess they made things difficult. I don't think it lasted long. And I'm sure they didn't have any children – I would've heard, if he had.'

Minnie's shaking her head. 'But what aboot the bairn, then? Who had the bairn, if it wasnae his wife?'

'A little girl, it was. The mother was one of the chambermaids at Dun – a young lassie herself, from a nice family. As far as we know there was no understanding between them, it was just one of these... a tragedy, really. It happened that year of the terrible snow. Do you remember that, Marion?'

'That snow? Oh my goodness, yes, that was... I was down in England though, with Aunt Tweedie. And that was the year my father died.'

'We heard afterwards Wull had appeared at Dun one night, near frozen, more dead than alive.' It's so matter-of-fact, the way Violet says it. So cut and dried, as if it didn't matter to her whether someone was more dead than alive. 'The lass put him in the barn and looked after him till he recovered.'

'Oh, dear God!' With my elbow on the arm of the chair and my head resting on my hand, I can shield my eyes.

'Then he up and off. Disappeared.'

'Oh, but he wouldnae hae left if he'd kent. I'm sure he would-nae hae done that.' She'd defend the devil, if he wasnae there to defend himself.

'So... what happened to the lass?' I think I'm striking an appropriate tone, but my voice is wavering.

'Kept her secret as long as she could, just told a friend when the baby started to come. But it went terribly wrong. The little girl was tiny – it was touch and go – and the mother haemorrhaged. They did send for a doctor, but she died before he could get to her.'

'That was a terrible thing.' Minnie's fidgeting. Her cheeks are red. 'But I still dinnae understand. Why did ye think I was that bairn?'

'The girl's family didn't want to know about the baby, so some-one took her to Cissy – was she in Dundee? I seem to remember it was Dundee. Anyway, Cissy took the baby in rather than have her sent to an institution.'

'She must hae died. My mum never mentioned nae bairn.'

The three of us avoid looking at one another, until Violet speaks.

'You... you don't have... you didn't find any papers, did you? When your mum died?'

'She'd nae papers. Said she'd lit the fire wi them ae nicht she'd nothing else tae burn.' Minnie's on her feet now, hands on her hips. 'Anyway, I'm no that wee girl. She must hae died. When was it, the Boer War? The 1890s? I wasnae even born then.'

'The Anglo-Boer War. 1900-1901. There were notices in all the papers at the time. Lord Lonsdale put together a force of 10,000 men. I don't know what on earth put it into Wull's head, but that's what he did, apparently. Trained at Cupar, sailed to South Africa and was never heard of again.'

'I was born December 1900.'

Mrs Jacob is still speaking, but I've heard enough. I wish she'd stop. I just wish she'd go. I need to think.

'And who knows what happened to Wull? I can't imagine him as a soldier. I've sometimes thought he might have deserted, made a life for himself, somewhere on the high veld. I've thought of him there, playing his fiddle.'

'He's nae daein that, oniewey. I hae the fiddle, under my bed. My mither aye kept it there, and I've just done the same.'

CHAPTER 20

Arbroath: June, 1946

The music puts me in mind o driftin in the mighty current o a river. At the rate Minnie's fingers flick through the pages o her book she's neither listenin, nor readin. She gets up and rattles the fire wi the poker and by the sound it's a shovel o dross she's put on. 'I've been thinkin aboot what Mrs Jacob said.'

It's an effort, to keep my eyes open.

'She wasnae even there. How would she ken the richt wey o daen? It was all 'maybe this' and 'maybe that'. Wi that poor wee lassie dead, how could they be sure? About Uncle Wull, I mean. Folk'll blame anybody… specially if they're no there tae defend themselves. And well, ye ken, if they're nae like ither folk.'

The face hovering above me looks a wee bit anxious. 'Ye've been gey lukewarm the day, have ye nae?' She raises my head to plump up the pillow. 'Can I talk tae ye, though?'

My attempt at a smile reassurance enough.

'Somewey or ither Marion, I just cannae get used tae the

idea.' The bed tilts as she sits on the edge. 'Aboot my mum, I mean.'

I let her understand I'm listening.

'That my mum wasnae really my mum. My dad now… well, I never kent him, did I? And I dinnae really care. But even so… Uncle Wull – my dad? No, she would've said. My mum would hae told me that. Why would she no just say, if that was the wey? I cannae see it.'

On the wireless the river twists and turns and carries me with it. Minnie sighs and stands up. 'Are ye fit enough tae gae through this stuff frae the sideboard? We'll hae tae dae it sometime.'

I'm past caring.

'I had a wee lookie. There's some linen, and this here.' She lifts the hat-box and sets it on my bed.

J. Renard, 70, Rue de la Montagne, Bruxelles.

And a picture of a fox. In the shop, Monsieur Renard flirted with me and with Margaret and he sat between us at the theatre. We laughed so much, when he'd gone.

Slight turbulence: swirls and eddies – nothin more than that – add a wee frisson to the music. I close my eyes for a second until I get my balance and my breath back.

'There's nae much in here,' she's saying. 'A wee bundle o yer books – a notebook, a big envelope… official like papers.' A rummage around. 'Aye, certificates in that. And there's a wee parcel.' She gropes into the corners. 'That's it. Will I just gae through them, then?'

I make a brusque gesture towards the fire.

'No.' She shunts them into a pile. 'I will not. Nae yet. I'll sort them first, mak sure there's nothing ye need.'

I hear the shufflin o paper, things bein set aside. 'Here's a sad wee poem', she says. 'This is ane I havenae seen afore.'

Seedpearls on Blackthorn

Ayont the bonnie braes o hame
Whaur wolves and thochts roam free
Moonlicht tinkled frae the sky
And fair enchanted me.

It fell upon a thorny bush –
Wi a hert black as the nicht
And blessed my care-worn een
Wi sic a bonnie sicht

Ayont the bonnie braes o hame
My life began anew
When true love fashioned me a ring
Wi beads o pearly hue.

The dawn it lent a lustrous glow
The dew a rainbow sheen
I had nae mind o prickly thorns,
Or whaur thae pearls had been.

An eagle and its mate soared high
Tae a hidden melody.
My true love handed me a ring –
But his hert he didnae gie.

'Feels like there's a wee bit missin. Did ye nae think so yersel?'
She pecks my forehead.

Ayont the bonnie braes o hame – clad in mists and memory –
On that road across the whinny moor towards Infinity
The breeze that maks the thorn bush moan is cheerless company.
I hear it sigh, year aifter year, 'Pearls are for tears', you see.

How could I explain? I say nothing, push my forehead against
her lips and let myself go wi the tide. The lilt of her voice merges
perfectly with the melody.

~

'Did I waken ye?' She's leaning right ower me, her breath on my
face. 'Look, this parcel is addressed tae Mrs Service. Never even
been opened. Posted 1936, it looks like. Whit wey would yer
sister nae hae opened it?'
    I never opened it either.
    'Nae often ye see wax seals nowadays.'
    She rolls up the string, folds the paper as she goes. 'Ye cannae
get a haud o nothin thae days.' A sheet of notepaper in her hands:
'It's got an official stamp – GARNAVEL HOSPITAL. "The enclosed
were left behind when you collected your sister's effects."'

The embroidered squares are held up for my benefit. 'Look at this. Look at it.' She sets them around me, within reach. 'Exquisite!' she says. 'Never seen nothin like it.'

My hand flutters on the quilt.

'There must be what... twenty squares?'

A garden of flowers – stylised, not to my taste, but I appreciate the heartache she put into them. Some unfinished – her eyesight gave out, in the end.

'Whit'll we dae wi them?'

She's a bit like Cissy in the way she likes to see things through. Maybe Wull too, who knows? A credit to the both of them.

'What aboot the kirk? That nice minister man, he's aye saying how they need tae raise funds, there's that many widows, and sodgers that cannae get jobs... the Guild's aye lookin tae raise money. Framed and raffled – think what they'd bring in!'

Ethel's mark on the world: her legacy.

'Maybe a shame tae split them up though.' She takes hold of my hand. 'Here, dinnae gae back tae sleep yet.'

She lifts my hand. A dried flower in an envelope is shaken onto my palm. The petals disintegrate as soon as they touch my skin. 'Och, never mind, it was just a wee flower. A copper coin in front of my face: 'And look at this, an auld Victorian penny.'

'You keep that,' I try to say, but it's hard to convey with fingers.

'And I've been through yer certificates. Ye never said ye'd a wee brither that died?'

M (initial of manslaughter) The brand of a person

convicted of that offence and admitted to the benefit of
the clergy. It was burnt on the brawn of the left thumb.

∽

It's a flat plonk, plunk, plonk, plunk that wakens me. My mouth's parched. There's a glass of water on the bedside table beside me, but I can't reach.

She puts the fiddle on the bed and dips a finger in the glass to moisten my lips. 'Marion, listen! I was richt! And if it hadnae been for you and that sideboard, I'd never hae thocht tae rake in Uncle Wull's fiddle case.

It wasnae South Africa he was gaein. Mrs Jacob was wrong. I found this thing… a kind o letter, frae a shippin company: "Allan Bros. (Liverpool and London)".'

The orchestra fades into the background as the theme is taken up by the violin again.

'Are ye awake? Marion, are ye listening? It was Canada. A sailin tae Canada. February 1900. There must hae been an understandin atween the twa o them. Twa berths, he had, Uncle Wull. Mr William Greig. Look.' Something is laid on my palm. 'Ye see? Twa berths. Ane o thae must hae been for the lassie he loved.' She takes it back and reads again. 'Just like I thocht. But I wonder whit happened that they never went?'

She takes my hand and holds it palm up. 'And this.' On my palm I feel the triangular shape, the weight, the worn-smooth-by-the-sea texture, of a shard of china. 'That must hae meant something tae him.'

'Elliot. ' I manage to get it out at last.

'What are ye sayin?' As she leans closer, her hair brushes against my face. 'Ye all richt, lovie? Elliot Sands, dae ye mean? Ye could be richt. It's the kind o thing ye'd pick up on a beach.'

The current's stronger now. Everything's on the move: patterns o music, o words, o water, fire, dust, against a silvery light. And everything's as it should be.

'Well! Would ye nae just wonder what the real story was?'

POSTSCRIPT

∼

The Courier and Advertiser, 17th April 2001

A striking piece of work, composed of seventeen large cream-coloured satinised squares, each one depicting a creatively imagined flower, each one embroidered with great skill, was unveiled this week in the Queen's Aisle of Brechin Cathedral.

The name of the original artist is not known, but thanks to an elderly member of the congregation, some of the facts about its history are known. The embroiderer was a lady. On her death, the squares were bequeathed to her housemaid, who retired to Brechin and became an active member of the congregation of the Cathedral. Not valuing her own skills as an embroiderer, she passed on the squares to the late Mrs Johnston of Airlie Street, probably in the 1950s, on the understanding that she would 'do something with them'. Unfortunately, Mrs Johnston was unable to complete them and they lay forgotten until last year, when they were handed, along with the original skeins of thread, to the ladies of the local branch of the Embroiderers' Guild. The ladies willingly took on the challenge of completing the squares, mounting and quilting the work.

On behalf of the cathedral, the Minister thanked the women for their efforts and assured them their work would, over the coming years, be an inspiration not only to the congregation but also to artists everywhere, that they should never lose hope their work will reach an appreciative audience.